Lila's Valentine's lie . . .

As Jake headed for the lunch line, Lila could feel all the Boosters gazing at her sympathetically. It was unbearable. She took a deep breath.

"Whew, what a relief!" she exclaimed, tossing her hair over her shoulder. "After I dumped Jake so hard last weekend, I thought he'd never speak to me again." Leaning back in her chair, she fanned herself with her clipboard. "I'm really glad he's decided to be big about it. I think dating someone else will definitely be good for him."

"What?" Jessica asked in a shocked tone. "You never told me you and Jake broke up."

Lila shrugged ruefully. "He asked me not to tell anyone," she lied. "You know how it is. I guess he felt embarrassed about it."

"Gosh, Lila, you really handled it well. He even seemed grateful that you didn't hate his guts or anything," Janet said admiringly.

"Yeah, well . . ." Lila said modestly.

"So why did you break up with him?" Jessica wanted to know.

Lila felt her heart sink. Why would I break up with Jake Hamilton? Why w̶o̶u̶l̶d̶ ever break up with him?

"Lila?" ░░░░░░░░░░░░░░░░░░░░░░░░ broke up."

Thin░░ ░░░░░░░░░░░░░░░░░░░░░░░░

"Oh, bec░░ ░░░░░░░░░░░░░░░░ aid coolly.

SWEET VALLEY TWINS
◇ SUPER EDITION ◇

Lila's Secret Valentine

◇

Written by
Jamie Suzanne

Created by
FRANCINE PASCAL

BANTAM BOOKS
NEW YORK · TORONTO · LONDON · SYDNEY · AUCKLAND

LILA'S SECRET VALENTINE
A BANTAM BOOK : 0 553 50314 6

Originally published in USA by Bantam Books

First publication in Great Britain

PRINTING HISTORY
Bantam edition published 1996

The trademarks "Sweet Valley" and "Sweet Valley Twins"
are owned by Francine Pascal and are used under license by
Bantam Books and Transworld Publishers Ltd.

Conceived by Francine Pascal

Produced by Daniel Weiss Associates, Inc,
33 West 17th Street, New York, NY 10011

Cover photo by Oliver Hunter

Bantam Books are published by Transworld Publishers Ltd,
61–63 Uxbridge Road, Ealing, London W5 5SA,
in Australia by Transworld Publishers (Australia) Pty Ltd,
15–25 Helles Avenue, Moorebank, NSW 2170,
and in New Zealand by Transworld Publishers (NZ) Ltd,
3 William Pickering Drive, Albany, Auckland.

Printed and bound in Great Britain by
Cox & Wyman Ltd, Reading, Berkshire.

To Anders Johansson

One

◇

"OK, take it from the top!" Janet Howell yelled during Boosters practice on Wednesday after school. Jessica Wakefield, along with the other members of the Sweet Valley Middle School cheerleading squad, quickly got into formation beside her.

Standing in a long line with their arms around one other, the Boosters did a series of cancan kicks.

"Give me an L! Give me an O! Give me a V! Give me an E! What's that spell?" they all yelled in unison. "What's that spell? Love! Love! Yay!" They finished with high-flying kicks to the center, then bounced up and down, shaking their pom-poms.

Jessica's heart was beating hard—as much from excitement as from the exercise. Valentine's Day was only ten days away, and she, along with practically everyone else at Sweet Valley Middle School, was really getting into the Valentine's Day spirit. She couldn't wait to perform the special Valentine's cheers the Boosters were practicing.

"That was great, you guys," Janet said. "Let's all take a water break."

Pushing her damp blond hair off her forehead, Jessica made her way to the water fountain at one side of the gym, the other Boosters following close behind her.

"This Valentine stuff is great, but I hate getting all sweaty," Tamara Chase said. As an eighth-grader, she was two years older than Jessica. She was also the tallest member of the Boosters Squad.

"But it's definitely worth it," Grace Oliver said. "These cheers are awesome."

"Yeah," agreed Lila Fowler, Jessica's best friend, as she flipped her long brown hair over her shoulder. "We should do them all year round, instead of just at Valentine's."

Grace shook her head. "But if we did them all the time, they wouldn't be special."

"Speaking of special," Janet said, coming up behind them, "have you all been working on your assignments?"

Jessica was glad to hear this question—she couldn't wait to show off the new cheer she had made up. This year the Boosters had come up with a totally fabulous Valentine's idea: For just two dollars, they would perform a special, personalized cheer for someone's Valentine. For instance, if Jim Sturbridge hired the Boosters to do a cheer for Belinda Layton, the Boosters would go to the front of the cafeteria at lunchtime and perform a cheer that had Belinda's name in it. And if Jim paid *four* dollars, the Boosters would write a new, unique cheer all about Belinda. Janet, as head Booster, had assigned each member of the squad to try to come up with one cheer that would work with a variety of names.

"I think I came up with something," said Winston Egbert, the only boy on the Boosters.

"OK, let's see it," Janet said.

Standing back a little, he raised his arms high up in the air and spread his feet apart. He did a series of knee lifts and kicks as he began his cheer. "Red is a rose, tulips are pink! Cover your nose, 'cause your feet sure do sti—"

"That's enough, Winston," Janet interrupted sharply. Jessica covered her smile with her hand. Winston wasn't exactly the coolest guy in sixth grade, but she had to admit he added some spice to Boosters practice.

"Now, this is serious, you guys," Janet said. "If we want to raise enough money to hire a professional photographer to take Valentine's portraits at the dance next Friday, we have to have some really good cheers, cheers that people will want to buy for their boyfriend or girlfriend. Now, who has a *real* cheer?"

She put her hands on her hips and looked around at the Boosters. Janet was not only the Boosters captain, she was also the president of the Unicorn Club, a group of the prettiest and most popular girls at Sweet Valley Middle School, and Jessica thought that she tended to be a little bossy.

"I've come up with one that I think is pretty great," Jessica said, walking to the middle of the gym and fluffing up her pom-poms. In honor of the holiday, the Boosters had switched from their usual dark-purplish-blue-and-white pom-poms to red-and-white ones. "It goes like this."

Raising one pom-pom over her head, Jessica did a grapevine to the left, then switched pom-poms and did a grapevine to the right. She did some low kicks as she chanted her cheer. "Valen*tine's* is coming *soon*, and you know what to *do*. Hmm-hmm sends me to the *moon*. Hmm-hmm, I love *you*! Yay!" She finished with a high split-kick. She landed and waited expectantly, proud of the way she had made everything rhyme.

Ellen Riteman looked at her blankly. "What's a *hmm-hmm*?" she asked.

Jessica let out a small sigh. "The *hmm-hmm* is the person's name," she explained patiently. "Like, just for an example, *Aaron* sends me to the moon. *Aaron*, I love *you*."

"Just for an example, huh?" Mandy Miller teased.

Lila and Ellen giggled. Everyone knew that Jessica and Aaron Dallas were sort of boyfriend and girlfriend.

"Yes, well, thanks, Jessica," Janet said briskly. "Good try. Anyone else got anything?"

Jessica looked at Janet in disbelief. *Good try? Good try? How about, "That was fabulous, Jessica"? How about, "Thank goodness we have Jessica's cheer"?* She shook her head. Some people just didn't recognize greatness when they heard it.

"I'll try," Kimberly Haver said, walking to the center of the gym. "I was working on this for a couple of couple hours last night." She jumped up and came down in a split, then leaped up and twirled around. "Give me a K! Give me an E! Give me an N! What's that spell? Ken! Be my valentine! Yay!" She bounced up and down, swinging her pom-poms.

"That's it?" Jessica asked. "You spell their name and say 'Be my valentine'?" *Good grief, it didn't even rhyme!* she thought.

Janet frowned. "Pretty lame, Kimberly," she said frankly. "And what if their name is really long, like Steven, or Patrick?"

"Or Jessica," Jessica pointed out, her arms across her chest. "Or Elizabeth." Elizabeth was Jessica's identical twin sister, but she wasn't a Booster or a Unicorn.

"OK, OK, I get the point," Kimberly said huffily, stalking over to sit on the bleachers.

"Anyone else?" Janet asked.

The Boosters were silent.

"I've been so busy with the decorations committee," Amy Sutton said meekly.

"We've had out-of-town guests," Tamara said, looking at the floor.

Janet crossed her arms. "Listen, you guys, we need cheers, and we need them now. Jessica's the only one who came up with something halfway decent."

Jessica smiled importantly, even though she thought her cheer was way more than halfway decent. In fact, she thought it was brilliant. And she was going to try to come up with at least one more.

"OK, let's take ten and try to work on some stuff, right now," Janet continued, clapping her hands. "Then we'll end for the day."

Jessica felt another flicker of excitement—and not just because of the cheers. Everything about Valentine's Day was thrilling to her this year. "I can't wait to see the Valentine's portraits," she said, turning to Lila, Mandy, and Amy. "It's totally grown up."

"And totally romantic," Lila said. "We'll be able to keep the pictures forever."

"Who gets to keep them?" Amy asked, looking concerned. "The girl or the guy?"

Jessica, Lila, and Mandy frowned in puzzlement.

"The girl," Jessica said firmly. "Guys don't care about stuff like that. But if they do, we could just have two pictures made."

"Good idea," Lila said.

"Anyway," Jessica continued excitedly, "I'm getting this great new dress. I saw it in the window at Bibi's yesterday at the mall."

"I'm still looking," Amy said. "It's hard to find something that isn't too sissy." Amy was a small, wiry tomboy who was Elizabeth Wakefield's best friend. Besides Winston, she was the only non-Unicorn to be accepted into the Boosters, and she didn't usually hang around with them outside of practice.

"How about you, Lila?" Jessica asked. Lila always wore the most beautiful and expensive clothes. Her father was one of the richest people in Sweet Valley, and as an only child whose parents had divorced when she was little, Lila tended to get pretty much anything she wanted.

"Oh, I really don't have anything that's right. I guess I'll have to find something new," Lila said airily.

"Five more minutes," Janet called from the other side of the gym several moments later.

"Whoa, we'd better get to it," Amy said. "I almost forgot we were supposed to be coming up with cheers. Do you have any good moves, Lila?"

"Hmmm?" Lila mumbled distractedly, staring into space. She couldn't think about cheers right now. All the talk about the Valentine's dance had made her wistful and dreamy. She pictured the whole night perfectly.

The streetlights would make eerie pools of light on the pavement outside the gym as middle-schoolers arrived in droves for the dance. But Lila would be nowhere in sight. It would be getting late. People would begin to whisper: *Where is Lila Fowler?*

Suddenly, a long, dark, chauffeured limo would pull up to the gym's doors. Everyone would turn to see, but the windows would be tinted and no one would be able to see in. Then, slowly, the door would open. One delicate foot wearing an adorable black suede platform shoe would emerge. With any luck at all, the night would be slightly foggy, like a scene in a music video. Then Lila would put down her crystal goblet of sparkling cider and slide gracefully off the leather seat. All the girls would gasp when they saw her beautiful, luxurious outfit. All the guys would stare, transfixed.

Then Jake Hamilton, who was just about the cutest guy in seventh grade, not to mention the whole school, would come around the car and take her hand. The girls in the crowd, especially the Unicorns, would whimper with envy. Jake would look totally fantastic in black jeans and a tuxedo shirt that was open casually at the neck. An untied bow tie would be draped around the collar, just like the one Joey Martin had worn on one of Lila's favorite TV shows, *42 Wilshire Road*. A fancy tapestry vest would be buttoned up almost all the way. Then, arm in arm, they would sweep into the gym as everyone in the crowd wished they looked one-tenth as hot as Lila and Jake, Valentine Couple of the Year. . . .

Lila smiled to herself at the image. Technically, she knew that she and Jake weren't actually a couple—yet. And he hadn't actually asked her to the dance—yet. But over the past couple of weeks, he had given her all sorts of signals, sending her love messages that only she could decode.

Such as the time they had both arrived at the water fountain outside Mr. Davis's homeroom, and Jake had stepped back to let her drink first. That had been pretty obvious. And just the other day, a line of students had been filing out the cafeteria door, and Jake had held it open while Lila walked through. Sure, he'd held it open while several other people had gone through, too, but it had been meant for her. She couldn't help it if those people had taken advantage of Jake's good nature.

Lila sighed dreamily. By now, practically everyone in school knew that Jake had a crush on her and she had a crush on him. And it was only a matter of time before he asked her to the dance.

"Earth to Lila, Earth to Lila," Jessica was saying, snapping her fingers in front of Lila's face. Lila came out of her fantasy with a jolt. Everyone was looking at her.

"Well, I can't tell you exactly what I'm wearing," she said hastily. "It's a surprise."

Mandy giggled. "Actually, Lila, that was a couple of subjects ago. We were supposed to be coming up with cheers, but I can see where your mind is."

Lila blushed and cleared her throat. "Yes, of course, cheers. I just think you can never talk too much about clothes," she said, recovering herself. "After all, this dance is super important. We, as Unicorns and Boosters, have to present the right image."

"I don't even know if I'll be going to the dance," Mandy said shyly. "I haven't been asked yet." Mandy and Peter Jeffries liked each other, but they weren't really going out or anything.

"Mandy, you *have* to have a date," Lila said, thinking about how she and Jake would be making everyone green with envy. "Anyone who's *anyone* is going as a couple. I know Patrick Morris has asked Sophia Rizzo, which is a miracle, and even Amy here has managed to snag Ken Matthews."

"Gee, thanks," Amy said dryly. "I guess that hypnosis must have worked on Ken."

Jessica and Mandy laughed.

"You know what I mean," Lila said impatiently. "We're in sixth grade now. Most people go to dances in couples."

"That's not true," Grace said, coming up to hear what Lila was saying. "I know lots of people who are going just as friends, or girls going together, or just guys."

Mandy looked at her gratefully.

Lila frowned. "Maybe going stag is OK for *some* people. But a *Unicorn* would never show up at the dance without a fabulous date."

Two

◇

"OK, then, it's agreed," Elizabeth Wakefield said at the after-school staff meeting of *The Sweet Valley Sixers*, the official sixth-grade newspaper, which she had helped found. "For this Friday's and next Friday's issues, we'll rent out space on the back page for valentine lovegrams."

"At a dollar fifty a pop," Julie Porter added, tucking a strand of wavy red hair behind one ear.

"Right," said Elizabeth. "And I've got another idea. Maybe some of us could help people write their lovegrams—like if they're not sure of what they want to say, or they're shy. For another dollar, we could write it for them."

"That's an excellent idea, Elizabeth," Mr. Bowman said approvingly. He was Elizabeth's English teacher and the faculty adviser for the

Sixers. "You could help people who aren't as gifted with words as you."

Elizabeth smiled. She loved writing, and she thought that working on the lovegrams would be a lot of fun.

"It really is a great idea," Sophia Rizzo agreed. "Between the money we raise, and what the Boosters will get from their cheers, we're going to be able to put on an incredible dance!"

"Yeah, but remember that we're donating only half our money," Julie said. "The other half we need to keep to help cover newspaper operating costs."

"OK, then, I think we're all set. This meeting is adjourned," Mr. Bowman said. "But if any of you need to stay late, I'll be here for a while."

Elizabeth checked her watch. The Boosters would be practicing for another ten minutes. She decided to wait around for Jessica so they could walk home together.

"Are you staying for a while, Elizabeth?" Julie Porter asked, gathering her books together.

"Yeah. The Boosters should be done soon."

"I'll wait with you—there are a few things I wanted to look up in the computer." Julie settled in front of the newspaper's computer and turned it on.

"I can't wait to tell Jessica about our lovegram idea," Elizabeth told Julie.

Julie smiled. "It seems like you guys always tell each other everything."

"Uh-huh, always." Elizabeth thought for a moment. "Well, almost always. Basically, we never keep secrets from each other—well, almost never," she corrected with a grin.

Although Elizabeth and Jessica looked just alike on the outside, with long blond hair, blue-green eyes, and a dimple in their left cheeks, they were very different on the inside. Elizabeth was four minutes older, and they joked that it had made her the more responsible, serious twin. Elizabeth loved school and did well in all her classes. She also loved working on the *Sixers* and hoped to be a journalist someday. In her free time, she liked to read a good mystery, play sports, or have long talks with her close friends, Amy Sutton and Maria Slater. Everyone at Sweet Valley Middle School knew they could always depend on Elizabeth.

Jessica, on the other hand, was much more interested in clothes, boys, and gossip than in her schoolwork. She hated studying and thought of school as the place to show off new outfits and hang out with her friends in the Unicorn Club.

But despite their differences, the twins were best friends.

Elizabeth opened up her backpack and pulled out a book of love poems by Elizabeth Barrett Browning. "I was thinking of doing something special for Todd for Valentine's Day," she confided to Julie. "I thought these poems would give me some inspiration."

Julie quickly flipped through the book. "Wow! These are so romantic," she said.

"I know," Elizabeth said, blushing a little. "Todd's been pretty nice lately." She and Todd Wilkins had known each other practically forever, but in the last several months they had started becoming a little more than friends. Sometimes he did silly, infuriating things—like rigging up a bucket of water to fall on her head—but he could also be really sweet and considerate.

"So he's been acting like a real, live Romeo, huh?" Julie said with a teasing smile.

Elizabeth blushed a bit more deeply. "I guess you could say that." Recently, Todd had played the role of Romeo in the middle-school production of *Romeo and Juliet,* and Elizabeth and Jessica had shared the role of Juliet. Whenever Todd and Elizabeth rehearsed together, there was definitely a romantic energy between them. *Yes,* Elizabeth thought, *Todd's really a great guy sometimes.*

"So what special thing are you going to do for him?" Julie asked.

"Good question," Elizabeth said. "I mean, I don't want to be *too* mushy or anything."

Julie looked thoughtful. "But isn't that kind of the point of Valentine's Day? It's the one day out of the year when you're *supposed* to say and do really mushy things."

Elizabeth laughed. "I guess you're right. It's neat that there's a special day just to tell your friends how much they mean to you."

Julie snapped her fingers. "I know. Maybe you should send Todd a lovegram in the *Sixers*," she suggested.

"I don't know," Elizabeth said thoughtfully. "Tons of people will be sending lovegrams. It isn't really special enough. And it isn't very private, either."

"I guess not," Julie agreed. "Everyone will be reading them and talking about them. Even if you make yours anonymous, people would probably still be able to tell you wrote it."

"Jessica would, that's for sure," Elizabeth said, rolling her eyes. "She knows me too well. And she'd probably blab it to the rest of the Unicorns, who'd manage to blab it all over school." Elizabeth loved Jessica, but she knew all too well that her twin had a big mouth.

Julie glanced at her watch. "I better get going. Good luck coming up with an idea. Let me know if you want to talk about it some more." She shut down the computer and stood up.

"Thanks," Elizabeth said. "I will."

As Julie left, Elizabeth started to get her things together. *If I were Jessica, all this love-and-Valentine's stuff would come more naturally,* she mused. But Elizabeth had never really bothered with romance before. It was only lately that Todd had started looking different to her.

Besides, everyone in the middle school seemed to be into Valentine's Day this year. *I guess the love virus has infected even me,* Elizabeth thought as she put her notebook into her backpack.

She frowned as she walked down the hall toward the gym. She really wanted to tell Todd how she felt. Usually, she was so good at putting her feelings down on paper, but for some reason the thought of Todd's valentine made her feel unsure of herself. She needed help—she needed ideas. Tonight when she got home, she would read over all the love poems she could find.

"So, who's signed up for lovegrams? Come on, you can tell me," Jessica asked as the twins were walking home a few minutes later.

"No one yet," Elizabeth said with a laugh. "Tomorrow's the first day we're taking orders. Do you think Aaron will send you one?"

"I don't know if lovegrams are really his thing," Jessica said. "But I have a feeling he'll commission a special cheer for me—maybe even a four-dollar one. That would be so great." She slung her purple backpack to her other shoulder as they crossed the street onto Calico Drive, where they lived. Purple, the color of royalty, was the official color of the Unicorn Club. Every Unicorn tried to wear something purple every day.

"Yeah. I think getting a lovegram *or* a cheer would be pretty great. Todd's been so nice lately, I almost think he'll do something romantic for Valentine's Day." Elizabeth felt a surprising pang in her stomach at the thought of Todd doing something really sweet for her.

Jessica grinned as they turned up their front walk. "Isn't it cool that we both have a Valentine? I mean, sometimes I have someone, but you and Todd are fighting, and sometimes you have someone, but I'm all alone. For once, the Wakefield twins are having identical romances."

"You're right," Elizabeth said with a smile as she unlocked their front door. "But what do you expect from Juliet and Juliet? Of course we're all caught up in romance."

Jessica slapped her a high five. "Thou dost know it!"

"So today at school we had thirty-five people sign up for lovegrams," Elizabeth said, serving herself some green beans. The Wakefields were eating in the dining room on Thursday night. "That means tomorrow's issue is completely sold out. I had to stay late just to help type all the messages."

Elizabeth was really pleased with how the lovegrams page had turned out. And it had been fun to help people with their Valentine's messages. Just hearing so many sending romantic messages to each other had made her feel happy. By the end of the day, she was totally overcome with Valentine's spirit. *Gosh, I'm becoming such a sap,* she thought.

"It sounds great, honey," Mr. Wakefield said. "Did you have a favorite lovegram, or is it a secret?"

Elizabeth grinned. "I guess since the paper will be out tomorrow, it doesn't matter if I tell you. My favorite was: 'Dark beauty with eyes of night, a smile like light of day. You I revere with all my might, until you say me nay. Happy Valentine's Day,'" she quoted solemnly, gazing off into the distance.

Mrs. Wakefield looked at her. "Good heavens," she said.

"I don't get it," Jessica complained. "Say me nay? What's that supposed to mean?"

"It means, 'Until you tell me no,' stupid," Steven said, taking a big gulp of milk. "Or, to put it in language *you* would understand: 'Until you, like, say, like, get lost, OK, babe?'"

Steven was the twins' fourteen-year-old brother. He was a freshman at Sweet Valley High, and one of his favorite things to do was tease his younger sisters.

"OK, so it's mushy," Jessica said, ignoring

Steven. "Got it. But who sent it to whom?"

"It's confidential," Elizabeth informed her, cutting a piece of tuna steak.

"Oh, come on, Lizzie, don't be such a goody-goody," Jessica protested. "You might as well tell me, since I'll find out tomorrow anyway. *Please*, tell me. *Please, please* . . ."

"First of all, I'm not a goody-goody," Elizabeth said, rolling her eyes.

"OK, you're not a goody-goody," Jessica agreed. "Now, who wrote it?"

"You promise not to blab to Lila or anyone tonight?"

"Promise," Jessica said, crossing her heart.

"OK, then—since you *will* find out tomorrow anyway—Patrick Morris sent it to Sophia Rizzo. She has dark hair and dark eyes. Get it?"

Jessica looked amazed. "Patrick Morris wrote *that*?"

"He didn't actually write it," Elizabeth explained. "He hired one of the *Sixers'* talented staff to write it for him. For only one dollar more."

Mr. Wakefield smiled at her. "And that talented staff member was . . ."

"Well, me," Elizabeth admitted with a smile. Actually, she had been kind of surprised when that little poem had popped into her head. It must have been the influence of all those romantic poems she'd been reading.

"Goodness, Elizabeth, I had no idea you could compose something like that," Mrs. Wakefield said.

Steven leaned toward Jessica. "Compose means 'make up,'" he whispered.

Jessica stuck her tongue out at him.

"Well, it sounds totally phony," Steven continued to Elizabeth. "Nobody talks that way."

Elizabeth sighed. "For your information, it's a love poem," she told him. "Lots of love poems sound like that—all exaggerated and old-fashioned. That's what makes them romantic."

"But I guess you wouldn't know anything about being romantic, would you, Steven?" Jessica said snidely. "I mean, you're the guy who gave Cathy Connors a wrench set for her birthday."

Cathy Connors was Steven's girlfriend. The twins had helped them get together in the first place.

"It was for her bicycle!" Steven said, defending himself. "She wanted it! I could tell she really liked it. It was a good set."

"Oh, please. She was just being nice," Jessica said, taking a bite of salad. "She was lying through her teeth."

"She was not lying!" Steven protested. "She loved it!"

"The poem was very nice, Elizabeth," Mrs. Wakefield broke in. "I'm just surprised Patrick was comfortable sending such an intense lovegram to Sophia."

"He wasn't at first," Elizabeth admitted. "But I managed to convince him. After all, it's Valentine's Day. Lots of people will be sending romantic lovegrams."

"So I guess that means Miss Smarmy will be in business," Steven muttered.

"Steven, enough," Mr. Wakefield said.

"Well, does anyone want to hear about the Boosters' special cheers?" Jessica asked, quickly jumping in. "Today at lunch we had ten people sign up for cheers. We'll start doing them next Monday and perform every day next week. And guess what? We're going to use the cheer I made up. Jim Sturbridge chose it to send to Belinda Layton."

"Is that the cheer I heard you working on in your room?" Elizabeth asked.

Jessica nodded, finishing up her rice. "We have five other basic cheers that we can put someone's name in," she said in a professional tone. "Some work with one-syllable names, and some with two or more syllables." She looked up and beamed. "It's a great feeling, knowing that the Boosters are helping true love along."

Steven leaned over his plate and made a gagging sound. His father shot him a warning look.

"I know what you mean," Elizabeth said, glaring at Steven. "Today, when people didn't know what to say to their valentines, I had a great time helping them come up with the right words. It's like we're unlocking their innermost feelings."

"Innermost feelings of nausea, maybe," Steven muttered. "In case no one's told you guys, you're in sixth grade."

"Shut up, Steven," Jessica snapped. "Just because you're totally lame when it comes to love—"

"OK, kids, OK," Mr. Wakefield said, tapping his spoon against his water glass. "I move we change the subject."

"I second it," Mrs. Wakefield said quickly. "Let's talk about something else."

"So how about those Lakers, huh?" Mr. Wakefield said energetically.

"Yes, they've really been hot lately, dear," Mrs. Wakefield supplied gamely.

Three

Later that evening, Elizabeth sat at her desk, staring at the open geography textbook in front of her. But she couldn't concentrate on homework—something more important was on her mind.

The phone rang, and Jessica called out her name.

Elizabeth got up, went out to the hall, and picked up the phone. "Hello?"

"Hi, Elizabeth. It's Amy. I'm trying to do the geography homework, but I can't concentrate."

Elizabeth giggled and carried the phone back to her room. "I know the feeling," she said. "I can't seem to focus tonight. I keep thinking about what to do for Todd for Valentine's Day."

"Hmm," Amy said. "How about a little present or something? Like a stuffed animal."

"I don't think so," Elizabeth said. "I wanted to

give him something more personal. I've been trying to write him a special Valentine's card, but I don't know, everything I write is so . . . so . . . lukewarm, I guess."

"Really? You were writing some great stuff today for other people," Amy said.

"Thanks. But it's easier to be mushy if you're writing for other people. All that romantic stuff isn't really *me*."

"Says who? You definitely showed your romantic streak today at the lovegram table," Amy said. "Maybe you're just locking yourself into your idea of what Elizabeth *should* be, instead of who Elizabeth really *is*."

Elizabeth laughed. "What TV talk show did you get that from?"

"I don't know. Vicki somebody," Amy admitted. "But it's true. Who says it isn't your style to be mushy? Who says you can't just let it rip?"

"Hmm." Elizabeth thought for a moment. Some of the Valentine messages she'd come up with today had been pretty romantic, she had to admit. She could still see Patrick's confused face as he read the message for his "Dark Beauty."

"Isn't it kind of, um, intense?" he had asked her skeptically.

But Elizabeth managed to convince him that it was OK to be a little on the intense side on Valentine's Day, and he had plunked down his dollar fifty.

Elizabeth frowned in concentration. True, a part of her really connected with all the love poems she'd been reading. They were so pretty. But she had a hard time imagining writing any of that stuff to Todd.

"I don't know," she said finally. "Lots of the poems I've been reading in books have been pretty over-the-top. Some of them have said stuff that I'd never say to Todd in a million years."

Amy giggled. "Like what, for example?"

"Oh, you know," Elizabeth said. "Stuff about worshiping the ground he walks on, loving him forever and ever. That sort of thing. I mean, I like Todd a lot and everything, but I don't know about worshiping the ground he walks on."

"Well, why don't you write him a card that says you like him a lot and everything?" Amy suggested. "That's pretty romantic."

Elizabeth laughed. "Maybe I'm worrying too much about this. I mean, he *has* been really sweet lately. Maybe I should just go for it and say something really sweet to him."

"Yeah, maybe you should," Amy agreed.

"What about you?" Elizabeth asked. "Are you doing anything special for Ken?" Ken Matthews and Amy were sort of boyfriend and girlfriend.

"Actually, I'm just thinking of getting him a regular funny card. Nothing too mushy. I think I'll leave the romantic stuff to you," Amy teased.

"I'll try not to let you down, then," Elizabeth joked.

But as she hung up the phone a few minutes later, she still wasn't sure what she should do. She noticed that her stomach felt funny—and she didn't think it was something she ate. It felt more like a case of valentines-itis.

A half an hour later, Elizabeth was staring once more at her geography textbook. She hadn't gotten beyond the third sentence of her assignment when the phone rang again.

"Hello?" she said, picking up the receiver.

"Elizabeth? It's Todd."

"Hi, Todd." Smiling, Elizabeth leaned back in her desk chair. She wondered if he somehow sensed she was thinking of him. Maybe they were such good friends now that their minds were almost linked. Elizabeth shook her head. *Good grief, what's happening to me?* she wondered. *I'm thinking more like Jessica every minute.*

"I'm calling to see if you're free tomorrow afternoon," Todd said. "*Exterminator Aliens from the Deep* is playing at the mall. I was thinking we could meet Ken and Amy there." Ken Matthews was one of Todd's best friends.

"That sounds fun," Elizabeth said happily. "We could all meet there after school."

"Yeah. And maybe we could get pizza first,"

Todd said. "I'll call Ken, and you call Amy."

"OK. I was just talking to her, but I'll call her back in a while."

"Great. I'll see you tomorrow at school," Todd said.

"Sounds good," Elizabeth said.

After hanging up, she flopped on her bed. Now she *really* couldn't study. Hearing Todd's voice made her stomach feel funny again. And this was the second time in two weeks that he had asked her to the movies. *He must be feeling kind of serious about me*, she thought happily.

Suddenly Elizabeth knew what she had to do. She and Todd had been getting along so well lately, she just had to let him know how much she enjoyed his friendship. And what better way than with a special Valentine's poem? Quickly, she got out a clean sheet of paper, then skimmed some of her favorite love poems for inspiration. Frowning in concentration, she began to write.

Finally, she sat back and read the final version. She let out a small gasp. The poem really didn't sound like her regular writing or speaking style at all. In fact, it sounded a lot like those old-fashioned love poems she'd been reading—kind of dramatic and emotional.

He'll be really surprised, she thought. *And also really touched, I bet.*

She put the poem inside her backpack so she'd

remember to take it to school. Tomorrow she would print it out nicely on the *Sixers'* computer, and then she would find a way to sneak it into Todd's locker.

"Has anyone gone for the four-dollar job yet?" Janet asked, sliding her lunch tray onto the Boosters cheer sign-up table on Friday. Lila and Grace shifted over to make room for her.

"Uh-uh." Tamara Chase shook her head. "But we have seven more of the two-dollar cheers."

"Wow," said Lila. "We won't have time to eat lunch next week, with all the cheers we'll be doing." She had been manning the sign-up table since the beginning of lunch period that day. She hadn't wanted to miss Jake when he came to request a cheer for her and to ask her to go to the dance with him. Quickly, she checked her appearance in her compact mirror. *Good*, she thought approvingly. Her lip gloss was still shiny.

Just then Rick Hunter, a cute seventh-grader, came up and requested a cheer for Kimberly Haver. Tamara took out an order form and wrote down the details.

Lila saw Jessica heading for the table.

"Who was that for?" Jessica demanded in a low whisper, leaning over the table.

"It was for Kimberly," Tamara said, gushing.

"Wait till she hears it!" Lila said. "I don't think she even knows he likes her."

"This is great," Jessica said, sliding into a chair and opening her carton of orange juice. "We get to find out all the latest news practically before it happens!"

She wiggled her eyebrows at Lila, and Lila laughed.

"So has Aaron requested a cheer yet?" Jessica whispered.

Lila shook her head, giving Jessica a sympathetic look.

"How about Jake?" Jessica asked meaningfully.

Lila shook her head again. "Not yet," she said, her brown eyes twinkling. Underneath the table, she crossed her fingers hopefully. Although the Boosters would still be taking orders next week, it seemed classier somehow to request a cheer before they actually started being performed.

"Well, don't look now, but here he comes," Tamara whispered.

As she watched Jake approach the table, Lila felt that she had just gotten on an elevator that was going down really fast. Her heart started pounding, and her palms were clammy. The next thing she knew, Jake Hamilton was leaning over the table, grinning at her.

"Hi, Lila," he said in his fabulous, husky voice.

Lila took in his sun-streaked, curly blond hair,

his blue eyes, his gorgeous smile. "Hi, Jake," she managed to get out.

"I wanted to order a cheer for next week," he said, putting his head close to hers confidentially. Lila could feel Jessica's elbow jabbing her gently in the ribs. She knew that the rest of the Boosters were staring at her, waiting to see what would happen. It was coming true—her fantasy. Here was Jake in the flesh, waiting to order an especially mushy cheer for her, just for her. Maybe he'd choose now to ask her to the dance next Friday, too. And best of all, her friends were there to see everything.

"Well, that's what we're here for," Lila said, striving for a casual tone.

"Do you want the basic or the extra-special?" Jessica asked, an expectant look on her face.

"The extra-special," Jake said, pulling four dollars out of his wallet.

Tamara took the money and got a new form to fill in his order.

"I want it to be for . . ."

Lila sat forward in her chair, a smile lighting her face as she gazed into his impossibly blue eyes.

"Brooke Dennis," Jake said in a conspiratorial tone.

Beside Lila, Jessica gasped, then smothered it behind her hand.

Tamara looked up with wide eyes, then quickly scratched out the *L* she had been writing. "Brooke

Dennis," she murmured, filling in the name.

Lila felt as though all the blood were draining from her face. *Brooke Dennis!* Brooke was also in sixth grade, and was tall and pretty. But still . . . what about all the signals Jake had been sending her? What about all those clues? What about her fantasy? How could Jake Hamilton come to this table looking so totally adorable and order an extra-special cheer for someone other than her?

Lila was considering sinking to the floor when she realized that the Boosters and Jake Hamilton were looking at her. *Get a grip*, she commanded herself. *You have an image to maintain*. She was a Fowler. Not only that, but she was a Unicorn and a Booster. She didn't need anybody, not even Jake Hamilton.

Lila flipped her hair over her shoulder and cleared her throat. "Sure thing, Jake," she said coolly. "But since you ordered the extra-special four-dollar cheer, you have to tell us what to say about Brooke."

"Well," Jake said smiling shyly, "could you talk about how pretty she is? Maybe say something about her dimples? And, um, mention that she likes peanut-butter cups?" He blushed, becoming twice as adorable as he had been moments before.

Lila felt a huge lump in her throat.

"And call her Snookie," Jake continued in a whisper.

Industriously, Tamara wrote down, "Nickname: Snookie."

"Okeydokey," Lila said brightly, checking the Boosters' schedule. "I think we have a slot open on Wednesday. Sound good?"

"Yeah," Jake said gratefully. "Thanks a lot, you guys."

"No prob," Lila said cheerfully.

Jake headed for the lunch line, and for a few moments no one stepped up to place a cheer order. Lila could feel all the Boosters gazing at her sympathetically. It was unbearable. She took a deep breath.

"Whew, what a relief!" she exclaimed, tossing her hair over her shoulder. "After I dumped Jake so hard last weekend, I thought he'd never speak to me again." Leaning back in her chair, she fanned herself with her clipboard. "I'm really glad he's decided to be big about it. Thank heavens he's picking himself up and moving on with his life. I think dating someone else will definitely be good for him. You know, help him put the pieces back together."

"What?" Jessica asked in a shocked tone. "You never told me you and Jake broke up."

Lila shrugged ruefully. "He asked me not to tell anyone," she lied. "You know how it is. I guess he felt embarrassed about it."

"Gosh, Lila, you really handled it well. He even

seemed grateful that you didn't hate his guts or anything," Janet said admiringly.

"Yeah, well . . ." Lila said modestly.

"So why did you break up with him?" Jessica wanted to know.

Lila felt her heart sink. *Why would I break up with Jake Hamilton? Why would anyone ever break up with him?*

"Lila?" Jessica pressed. "I asked why you broke up."

Think, Lila, think.

"Oh, because of Gray, actually," Lila said coolly.

Four

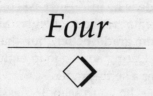

"Gray?" Janet was wide-eyed.

"Uh-huh." Lila's mind was racing. "Gray. Gray, uh . . . Williams."

"Who's Gray Williams?" Jessica asked, leaning forward.

Lila pushed her hair behind her ear and let out a short laugh, hardly knowing what she would say next. "We met—last Saturday. I was on my way home from the country club, and all of a sudden I saw this skateboard headed right at me, rolling down the sidewalk. So I stopped it with my foot." Lila was amazed at how clearly she could see herself in the scenario she'd just made up. She pictured herself standing on the sidewalk in front of the huge Fowler mansion. She saw herself put out one slim, sneakered foot to stop a wide, dirty skateboard. "Then this guy ran up to get it." Lila looked off dreamily into space. *Wow, this lying business is becoming really easy,* she thought. "It was Gray."

The Boosters drew a collective gasp.

"What grade is he in?" Janet asked.

"Eighth," Lila replied quickly. She liked the sound of ninth grade better, but that was totally unbelievable. Dating someone in eighth grade was pretty good for a sixth-grader.

"Where does he go to school?" Jessica wanted to know.

"Um . . . Lovett Academy." It was an exclusive private school across town. Lila figured that the Unicorns wouldn't be likely to know anyone from there.

"So what does he look like?" Tamara asked breathlessly.

Lila closed her eyes and pictured her dream guy. He was gorgeous—even more adorable than Jake. She took a deep, wistful breath. "Gray has slightly wavy dark-brown hair, with a touch of reddish gold in it," she said. "His eyes, oh, his eyes are a deep, beautiful green. Like the leaves in a forest." Lila looked around quickly to see if she was pushing things too far. Jessica was practically falling out of her seat, and Janet had her hand over her chest as if her heart were about to burst out of it.

"He sounds like—like a movie star," Grace Oliver said in an awestruck tone.

Lila shrugged. "Yeah, I guess he does kind of look like a movie star or a male model or something," she said casually.

"Was it an instant attraction?" Janet asked, eager for every detail.

Lila giggled softly. "Well, I guess it was for Gray," she said modestly. "For me, it was love at second sight. After all, I had Jake to consider."

Jessica and Janet nodded knowingly.

"But that very day Gray took me to get ice cream at Casey's," Lila said, really getting into the swing of things. "He ordered a coffee Heathbar-crunch cone."

Janet looked at her admiringly—coffee was a totally grown-up flavor. Most of the Unicorns hated it.

"And I realized that Gray was ten—no, a hundred—no, a thousand times cuter than Jake," Lila said rashly. "Plus, he was completely nuts about me, just like that." She snapped her fingers. "I told him about Jake and me, and it made him crazy. In fact, he threatened to do something drastic if I didn't immediately break up with Jake and go out with him instead." When she finished, she felt kind of shocked with how the story had ended up. Gray sounded like a real live wire.

"Oh, Lila, how romantic," Tamara simpered.

Lila twisted a strand of hair around her finger and smiled a secret smile.

"Only you could pull off something like this," Janet said approvingly. "And Jake doesn't even hate you for it. You have him eating out of your hand."

Lila grinned modestly.

"Geez, cuter than Jake," Jessica mused, shaking her head. "Whoa."

Lila smirked.

"Love at first sight," Grace said, sighing. "Like a fairy tale."

Lila gloated.

"Gosh, I just can't wait to meet him," Jessica said excitedly. "Is he going to pick you up for the dance, or will you go in your dad's limo?"

Lila went pale. *The dance. Oh, no!*

Elizabeth glanced at the clock hanging on the wall in the *Sixers* office. Twenty minutes left of lunch period. If she hurried, she could slip her note into Todd's locker and still have time to wolf down a sandwich in the cafeteria.

Tapping her foot anxiously, she watched as the computer printer slowly churned out a single sheet of paper. Elizabeth snatched it up and quickly scanned it.

She smiled in satisfaction. She had come to school early this morning and designed Todd's valentine on the computer they used for the newspaper. It was in fancy script lettering and had curlicues and other designs all around the edges. *It's beautiful*, she thought.

She was about to sign her name, but then she stopped. *It'll be more romantic if I send it anonymously. Besides, Todd will know it's from me right away. Who else would go to so much trouble over a poem for him?*

She quickly folded the poem, stuck it in an envelope, and sealed it. Then she wrote Todd's name on the front, and feeling excited and a little silly at the same time, kissed the back of the envelope right at the seal. Her pale lip gloss left a kiss mark.

Whew, she thought. *Todd isn't going to know what hit him.*

Tucking the envelope under her blouse, Elizabeth headed into the hall and down the stairs. Todd's locker was in the East Wing, and Elizabeth could get there without being seen by cutting through an empty eighth-grade chemistry lab.

So far, so good, Elizabeth thought, poking her head around the corner to the East Wing locker banks. She began to make her way down to Todd's locker, which was right in the middle of the hall. About five or six seventh-grade girls were heading down the hall toward her. They were laughing and giggling and talking about staying up late to see Johnny Buck on *Midnight Interview* that night.

Elizabeth reached Todd's locker and was about to slip the large white envelope through one of the air vents when she suddenly saw Todd himself coming down the hall. He was whistling and tossing a baseball in the air as he walked. Elizabeth ducked down, looking for a place to hide. She would die if he saw her with his valentine! It had to be a surprise. He had to find it in his locker when she wasn't around or the whole effect would be ruined.

Elizabeth breathed a sigh of relief as the crowd of girls stopped directly in front of Todd's locker, effectively screening her from Todd's view. She hunched down lower, pretending to fiddle with a combination lock. *Please don't come to your locker, Todd,* she begged silently. *Not yet.*

"I just can't wait till tonight," one of the girls said excitedly. "I hope I can stay up that late."

"Midnight is early," another girl scoffed. "I'll call you to make sure you're up."

"My brother always eats ice when he wants to stay awake," a third girl offered. "He just sits there and crunches his way through a bowl of ice cubes."

"That's disgusting," the first girl said.

"Well, it works," the third girl insisted. "Once when he wanted to stay up late to study for a test, he emptied out the whole icebox."

Elizabeth peeked over their heads and saw Todd whistling his way down the hall. He hadn't even glanced at his locker. She breathed another sigh of relief and straightened up as he disappeared around the corner. The girls also started walking again, leaving Elizabeth alone in the hall, envelope in hand.

Whew, that was close, she thought. *Thank goodness those girls showed up at the right time.* Hastily, she pushed the envelope into Todd's locker, then took off down the hall. A lighthearted feeling flowed through her as she headed to the cafeteria. She wished she could see the look on Todd's face when he read the poem. Maybe he would mention it this afternoon at the movie. Maybe he would get all mushy and hold her hand, and they could share a drink with two straws.

A sudden thought made her stop in her tracks, right in front of the cafeteria doors. Maybe he would even try to kiss her, in the dark theater.

A delicious shiver went down her spine. She really hadn't meant to kindle *that* much of a fire with her valentine love poem. But if she had, she would face the consequences.

Finally, Todd thought when the bell rang, signaling the end of his last class. He'd been looking forward to seeing *Exterminator Aliens from the Deep* all day. As soon as he got his books, he would meet Elizabeth, Amy, and Ken by the bus stop.

He gathered his books and strode quickly to his locker. When he opened it, a large white envelope fell out. Figuring that it was probably an announcement about a club meeting or something, he slipped it into his jacket pocket, hurriedly grabbed some books, and headed for the exit doors. Right before he pushed through the doors, he decided to see what was in the envelope. *It could be something about a homework assignment some teacher forgot to announce*, he thought.

The white envelope had "Todd" printed on it in large, fancy letters. It was surrounded by small red hearts. *An early valentine from Elizabeth*, he realized. His eyes crinkling with pleasure, Todd leaned his backpack against the wall and ripped the envelope open. Inside was a single sheet of paper, folded three times. He brushed it flat with his hand. Around the edges, there was a pretty border flowers and ivy. In the middle of the page was a poem.

Dear Todd,
I've often wished that I could show
How you pierced my heart with Cupid's bow,
But we've been friends for far too long
For you to buy my siren's song.

Oh, Todd, so deep your eyes of brown.
I pray I see our friendship's grown.
I pray I see your understanding
For the love my heart's commanding.

On this, the feast of Valentine,
Please say your heart feels just like mine.

With wings of air I look ahead
Toward a day with joys unsaid,

And then I'll know we two won't part
Because I've given you my heart.

With love from . . .

For long seconds, Todd just stared at the paper in his hand. Then he brushed his hair off his forehead and read the poem again. Could *Elizabeth* have written this? It had to have been her. Who else would send him a valentine?

Todd leaned against the wall, staring at the poem in amazement. No one but Elizabeth would be sending him a valentine, but . . . this poem sure didn't sound like her. It was so . . . serious. So devoted. So romantic. Elizabeth was really nice, and a good friend, but she didn't exactly spill her emotions all over the place like some other girls. It was one of the things he liked about her. She was a lot of fun but also so . . . sensible. Really pretty, but not all hung up on herself.

But if it hadn't come from Elizabeth, who was it from?

Todd's eyes widened. He must have a secret admirer! Somebody at Sweet Valley Middle School must have a crush on him. A big crush, if this poem was anything to go by. Feeling almost dazed, he wiped his hand across his forehead. Then he quickly folded the poem and stuck it into his backpack. He had to get going, or he would be late meeting Ken, Amy, and Elizabeth for the movie.

At the thought of Elizabeth, he frowned. She probably wouldn't like it if she knew he'd gotten a valentine from someone else. *But that's not exactly my fault*, he reasoned. He couldn't help it if someone, some girl, had totally fallen for him.

The question was, what was he going to do about it?

Five

◇

Good grief, what am I going to do? Lila sat on the gilt bench in the foyer of the Fowler mansion. It was a clear, beautiful Saturday morning, but if the weather had matched Lila's mood, it would have been dark and pouring rain outside. She had hardly slept a wink the night before, worrying about the Gray situation.

Well, it hasn't gone that far yet, Lila consoled herself. If she backed out of it now, there would be no harm done. After all, it wasn't as if she had hired some stranger to pretend to be Gray or anything. She laughed wryly at the thought.

Yeah, I'd better lose Gray now, she decided. Over the next day or two, she would pretend to start finding things wrong with Gray, and by Tuesday, they would be "broken up." Then she could just go to the dance alone and not worry about it. That would be the simplest thing to do.

The French doors at the other end of the foyer banged shut as Mrs. Pervis, the Fowlers' housekeeper, came bustling into the room. Her arms were full of freshly cut flowers.

"Oh, Lila, there you are," she said, sounding flustered. "Could you put these in water, please?" She thrust the flowers toward Lila.

Lila frowned. "I'm waiting for the Unicorns," she said. "We're going to the mall." She really didn't feel like fussing with the flowers and getting her hands all messy.

"Please do it," Mrs. Pervis pleaded. "Mr. Pratt, the gardener, has hurt his back, and I need to take him home. He was in the middle of cutting these flowers."

"Oh, all right." Lila sighed and rose to her feet. Mrs. Pervis handed her the bunch of flowers, and Lila headed toward the kitchen. "Did Mr. Pratt hurt himself badly?" she remembered to ask. Her father always said that good employers made good employees.

"I don't know," Mrs. Pervis said, gathering up her purse. She looked worried. "He's getting on in years." Then she bustled out the back door toward the garage. Moments later, Lila heard them drive away.

She dumped the flowers on the kitchen counter,

then found a large vase and filled it with water. She had just started arranging the flowers in the vase when someone tapped on the French doors leading to the patio. It was Janet, and with her were Jessica, Tamara, and Ellen. Lila went to let them in.

"Hey, guys," she said. "I'll be ready in a moment."

"Those flowers are gorgeous," Ellen said, leaning over to inhale deeply. "I love white roses." Ellen was Lila's best friend after Jessica.

Lila stuck a few more blooms in the vase, then stood back to examine the effect.

Janet moved closer to examine the bouquet. "They're beautiful, Lila. Are they from Gray?" she asked. She looked at Lila enviously, and Lila felt her heart leap from excitement. Everyone wanted to be the object of Janet Howell's envy. Even though Lila and Janet were first cousins, Janet often lorded her position as head Booster and president of the Unicorn Club over Lila.

"Yeah, they're from Gray," Lila said casually. "They just arrived. They're nice, huh?"

"They're more than nice," Jessica burst out. "They're fabulous! I've never seen such gorgeous flowers. They must have cost a fortune. You're so lucky, Lila."

"Gray's a sweetie," Lila said modestly, tucking the last bit of baby's breath among the lilies and carnations. She was vaguely aware that she was sinking deeper into a problem she would definitely have trouble getting out of later. But for now she loved the idea that the Unicorns were simmering with envy and admiration. They didn't need to know that the flowers really came from the Fowlers' garden.

Elizabeth glanced at Todd over the edge of her soda. It was Saturday at noon, and they were having a bite to eat at the Dog House, in the new food court at the mall. They had been together practically all morning, and he still hadn't mentioned finding his special valentine card. Elizabeth hoped that it hadn't gotten stuck between his books or, worse, that she had somehow put it in the wrong locker. She frowned, thinking back. No, it had definitely been the right locker.

Yesterday after school, when they had met Ken and Amy at the movies, Elizabeth had thought that Todd wasn't saying anything because he wanted to wait till they were alone. But even when Ken and Amy were getting popcorn and drinks, he hadn't mentioned it or gotten mushy. He hadn't held her hand. He had definitely *not* tried to kiss her in the dark movie theater.

Now they were totally alone and he still wasn't saying anything. She wondered what was on his mind.

"How's your Sled Dog?" she asked him.

Todd jumped a little, as though she had startled

him. "Oh, it's fine," he said. "How's your . . ." He looked at her plate. "Your French Poodle?"

"It's good," she answered. What was wrong with him? Not only was he not mentioning the card, he was being positively weird. He was really quiet and was hardly even looking at her. And he kept jumping every time she spoke. She wanted to ask him what was going on, but she knew it was his place to mention the card.

Elizabeth sighed. Romance could be very confusing sometimes. But Todd was a good friend, and she was sure that everything would work out eventually. She would just have to wait it out. Maybe the card had overwhelmed him, and he was still searching for the right words.

Elizabeth ate a french fry, trying to think of something they could talk about. "That movie was really fun yesterday, huh?" she asked lightly.

Again Todd looked startled. "Uh, yeah. Yeah, it was great," he muttered, looking down at his plate. He reached for his drink and took a big gulp.

"I liked it when the aliens pretended to be trick-or-treaters to get into that sorority party," Elizabeth continued.

Todd nodded, not looking at her. "Yeah. That was funny."

Elizabeth finished her last french fry and took a sip of her drink. Something was definitely going on with Todd. Something completely weird.

*   *   *

"This is totally hot!" Janet exclaimed, holding up a crinkled rayon mini-dress that had huge sunflowers printed all over it. It had a scoop neckline and long, flowing sleeves.

"Check it out!"

The Unicorns were trying on clothes at Bibi's, one of their favorite boutiques at the mall. All of the coolest juniors and seniors from Sweet Valley High shopped there.

"It's great," Ellen agreed. "But is it dressy enough? It looks a little cazh, you know?"

"You're right," Janet said thoughtfully. "But maybe I'll get this just for school and get something *else* for the dance."

"Hey, Lila," Jessica called, "what do you think?"

Lila went over to where Jessica was standing outside a fitting room. She was wearing a flowing, romantic mini-dress. Its cream background and pink floral print brought out the green of her blue-green eyes.

"It's you," Lila said, examining the dress critically. "And it's so right for the dance."

"Hmm, I think you're right." Jessica examined her reflection with a pleased expression. Then she looked up at Lila. "Have you found anything yet?"

Lila shook her head. Normally, she had no trouble finding clothes that she loved, but she was having a hard time mustering up the energy for this shopping trip. She couldn't get Gray off her mind. Or rather, she couldn't get the nonexistence of Gray off her mind. She knew she had to lose Gray fast— the dance was less than a week away. But so far she'd only managed to make their relationship sound like the romance of the century.

"Well, come see this," Jessica said, pulling Lila over to a rack of clothes. "I saw this and thought of you. Look." Jessica pawed through the outfits in the size-two area, then triumphantly pulled one out.

Lila almost gasped. It was exactly the outfit she'd been thinking of, the one from *Teen Scene* magazine. The top was a sophisticated black velvet bodysuit. Displayed with it were long hiphuggers with huge bells at the bottom. The fabric was dark, flowing, almost sheer. Lila knew that everyone else at school would be wearing a dress. No one else would dare to wear an outfit this dramatic to a dance. No one else could pull it off. No one but Lila.

"I love it, I love it, I love it," she murmured, reaching out to stroke the fabric.

Ellen came up and drew in a deep breath. "Lila, that is so fabulous. You have to get it."

Lila looked at the price tag. Inwardly, she gasped. It cost much more than she had ever spent on one outfit in her life. Her dad was usually pretty cool about her clothing allowance, but she didn't know what he would say about this—especially if, dateless, she didn't even go to the dance that she supposedly bought it for.

"Oh, my gosh, wait till Gray sees you in that," Janet said, sounding almost awestruck. "It's going to knock his eyes clean out of his head."

"He's going to feel like the luckiest guy alive," Jessica agreed.

Lila felt a flutter of pleasure. *Eat your heart out, Unicorns,* she thought, draping the outfit over her arm and heading to the checkout counter.

"I'll take it," Lila said, handing it to a saleswoman and pulling out her credit card.

What in the world is Todd doing? Elizabeth thought, watching him out of the corner of her eye. They were in Book Village, where Elizabeth was buying the latest Amanda Howard mystery. Todd was pretending to look through a new calendar featuring famous basketball players, but what he was really doing, Elizabeth realized, was watching other girls.

Todd swiveled his head as a girl their age walked by. His eyes stayed locked on the girl until another girl ambled past. Then his head snapped around to follow *her*.

This is so weird, Elizabeth thought. She knew that lots of guys probably girl-watched, but Elizabeth had never seen Todd do it before.

Elizabeth sighed as she got in line to buy her book. *Well, I guess maybe even Romeo girl-watched a little bit. It's a good thing I'm secure in this relationship, or this would really weird me out.* Elizabeth pulled out her wallet and paid for the book, then got Todd, and they left the bookstore.

As they strolled down the mall corridor, Elizabeth spotted Jessica outside a clothing boutique. "Look, there's Jessica," she said, pointing across the wide corridor at her sister. "Followed by a bunch of Unicorns, as usual."

Instantly Todd's eyes locked on to the group of girls, and he stared at them as though he'd never seen them before.

"I guess Jessica is going to the dance with Aaron," Elizabeth plowed on. "He hasn't asked her yet, but she's sure he will." Elizabeth wasn't used to dropping hints like this. And ordinarily, it wouldn't really have bothered her that Todd hadn't officially asked her to the dance—Elizabeth would have been just as happy to go with a group of friends. But for some reason, this year Valentine's Day seemed like a huge event to Elizabeth. Maybe it was all the romantic poetry she'd been reading. Maybe it was that she'd just been in *Romeo and Juliet*. Maybe it was because just about everyone she knew was sending lovegrams or cheers to their valentines. But whatever the reason, she knew that she'd been hoping for a better response from Todd.

Todd glanced at her. Elizabeth watched in amazement as he flushed uncomfortably. Then he looked away and began tracking other girls again. *This is unbelievable*, Elizabeth thought, starting to get exasperated.

"I talked to Olivia Davidson yesterday," Elizabeth continued, feeling as though she were speaking to a brick wall. "She's on the decorations committee for the dance. It sounds like they're planning all sorts of great stuff. We probably won't even recognize the gym. Next Friday. At the dance."

"Oh, gosh, what time is it?" Todd said suddenly, looking down at his watch. "Wow, one thirty. I better run. I have to go do . . . this thing." He spoke quickly, not really meeting Elizabeth's eyes.

"What do you have to do?" Elizabeth asked, confused. He hadn't mentioned this earlier.

"I have to go home and do something. For my mom. Yep. Well, gotta run. See ya, Elizabeth. I'll see you . . . at school, on Monday. Bye." And then he was gone, practically running away from her down the wide corridor of the mall. Elizabeth stared after him, feeling dazed.

What's going on? Why hasn't he mentioned my poem? Why hasn't he asked me to the dance? Why is he acting so strange?

Totally bewildered, Elizabeth sank down on a nearby bench. She was right across from a card shop. The windows were plastered with huge Valentine's displays.

Suddenly, an idea came to her. Maybe Todd was being so weird because he felt as if he hadn't done enough to deserve Elizabeth's poem. In fact, maybe he was completely overwhelmed by how nice her poem had been, and how much trouble she had taken over it, and now he felt unworthy. So maybe now he had run off to get something really nice for her for Valentine's Day, sort of to even the score.

Elizabeth blushed, feeling a little embarrassed by her thoughts: What was with her? She'd never been boy-crazy. Jessica usually handled that department. But here she was, getting hysterical over Todd Wilkins.

Still, the more she sat there thinking about it, the more Todd's behavior made a funny sort of sense to her. Her card had overwhelmed him. Now he had probably gone to order her some flowers, or maybe even to write his own love poem back. Elizabeth blushed again. She would probably go to school on Monday and find it in her locker.

Feeling much better, Elizabeth got up and headed toward the mall exit, swinging the bag with her new book in it.

"Elizabeth—wait up," someone called as she was almost at the exit.

Elizabeth turned to see Aaron Dallas running up to her. She smiled at him.

"I have to talk to you about something," Aaron said, panting. "Come on, let's go sit over here, where Jessica can't see us."

Where Jessica can't see us? Her eyebrows raised, Elizabeth followed Aaron to a nearby bench. This was turning out to be one of the weirdest days ever.

Six

◇

"So did you see Gray over the weekend?" Jessica asked Lila as they walked up the school steps on Monday morning.

This is your chance, Lila told herself. *Tell her you and Gray broke up.*

She turned to face Jessica, who was looking at her intently, almost eagerly. Lila couldn't tell what Jessica would rather hear: a wonderful, romantic story about Lila's weekend with Gray or a story of miserable heartbreak. After all, Jessica and Lila were very competitive with each other, even if they were best friends. And Jessica was still waiting impatiently for Aaron to ask her to the dance and commission a cheer for her. *She's probably dying for me to say we broke up*, Lila thought.

"Oh, yes, we saw each other," Lila murmured, smiling dreamily.

"What did you guys do? Did you tell him about the outfit you bought for the dance?" Jessica twirled the combination of her locker as she watched Lila's face.

"We just . . . hung out. Watched some TV. No, I didn't show him the outfit." Lila tried to sound casual. "I want it to be a surprise."

"What's a surprise? Ellen Riteman asked, coming up behind them, her arms full of her morning textbooks.

"Lila's outfit, for Gray," Jessica explained. "Boy, I can't wait to see his face when he sees you in that." She shook her head.

"Lila, I've been meaning to ask you," Ellen said as they headed toward their homeroom. "Do you think . . . well, does Gray maybe have a friend that *I* could go to the dance with?" She sounded hopeful. "I haven't been asked yet, and a cool guy like Gray probably has adorable friends." She put her hand on Lila's arm. "Will you at least ask him about it? I'd really appreciate it."

Lila started to feel a little sick. "Um, uh . . . well, I can *ask* him. I'm not making any promises, though. Most of his friends probably date girls from Lovett Academy."

Ellen looked at her gratefully. "Oh, thanks, Lila! You're the best. Even if nothing comes of it, you're so great to ask him. Thanks a lot." Beaming, she turned and ran off to her homeroom just as the bell rang.

Don't thank me, Lila thought guiltily. *Believe me, I don't deserve it.*

"He didn't say a word?" Amy asked Elizabeth, her eyes round with disbelief, as they sat hunched over their books in the library.

Slowly Elizabeth shook her head. She felt thankful that she and Amy had the same study hall period. Elizabeth normally used the period to study, but today she was anxious to sort out the Todd dilemma.

"We spent the whole morning together on Saturday," Elizabeth said in a low voice. "Then he suddenly ran off. And he didn't call me that night or yesterday. And this morning I checked my locker, but there was nothing there."

"And he hasn't asked you to the dance?"

Elizabeth shook her head. "It's only five days away. Four, not counting today."

"Well," Amy said firmly, "I'm sure he'll do it today. I mean, you might not get your official valentine until the actual day, but I'm sure he'll ask you to the dance soon. He knows he has to. After all, Ken asked me last week, and you know those two usually do things alike. Try not to worry."

Elizabeth forced a brave smile. "I'm trying. Now

I know how Juliet felt when she told Romeo that she loved him, and she wanted to marry him, and then she had to wait for him to answer her."

Amy nodded wisely. "Except you don't want to marry Todd," she pointed out. "And you didn't actually say that you loved him." For a second, she looked worried. "Or did you?"

"Oh, good grief, no," Elizabeth said quickly. "We're just, you know, friends. Like we always were. I just want to have a fun Valentine's Day, that's all."

"Hmm. Speak of the devil," Amy murmured, gesturing with her shoulder toward the door.

Elizabeth followed her glance and saw that Todd had come into the library. He looked around, then smiled a little when he saw her. As she watched him, he walked past her table and down one long row of stacks. Then, hidden from most people's view, he beckoned to her.

Amy winked at Elizabeth. "This is it! It's really romantic of him to follow you into the library. I'm sure he's planning to ask you to the dance now."

Elizabeth smiled. "I hope so," she whispered, her heart beating hard. She got up and casually drifted over to the tall bookshelves where Todd was hidden. She hoped Ms. Luster, the librarian, wouldn't wonder why Elizabeth was wandering around when she should be studying. Trailing her finger along a row of books, Elizabeth pretended to be searching for a certain title in the biography section. A few minutes later she was whispering hello to Todd.

"Hey," he said, looking just as uncomfortable as he had on Saturday at the mall.

It's probably hard for a guy to ask a girl out for something as important as a Valentine's dance, Elizabeth thought sympathetically. Her part was easy. At home, she had already practiced her response in the mirror: "Yes, Todd, I'd really like that," accompanied by a big smile. It was friendly and enthusiastic but not phony.

Todd looked around to see if anyone was nearby, and Elizabeth smiled at him encouragingly.

"Uh, Elizabeth, I was wondering . . ." he began, looking off at the rows of biographies.

"Yes, Todd?" she prompted softly.

"I was wondering, that is, I think . . ."

Poor guy, Elizabeth thought tenderly. *This is really tough for him.* She smiled at him again.

"I think, um, that maybe we should take it easy for a while," he muttered.

Elizabeth's mind went blank momentarily. "Take it easy?" she repeated in confusion. "What do you mean?"

"I mean, maybe we should see other people," Todd blurted, then quickly lowered his voice. "You know, not be so . . . serious."

Elizabeth tried to control her gasp. Since when

did going to the movies two weekends in a row count as serious? "Let me get this straight," she said, struggling to keep her voice down, feeling her heart begin to pound. "You're breaking up with me—four days before Valentine's Day?" *And after that nice poem I sent you?* she wanted to add. But she didn't. She wouldn't lower herself to remind him of that.

"Well, not breaking up, exactly," Todd said, shifting from foot to foot. "Just, you know, I want to take it easy. You know, see other people."

Elizabeth stared at him blankly while he looked more and more uncomfortable. *How could he do this after I said all those nice, romantic things to him?*

Suddenly, Elizabeth had a flash of insight. Todd had obviously misunderstood her valentine poem. He thought she was madly, crazily in love with him, and he was terrified. All she did was send him one slightly . . . ardent note, and he was freaking out. Running for his life. Bailing out.

She firmly set her jaw. *Fine*, she thought. If he was such a wimp as to be scared of a little sincere emotion, that was his problem. And if he was so full of himself as to think she actually worshiped the ground he walked on, just because she was sweet enough to send him an old-fashioned Valentine's Day poem, well, then he was just a jerk. She wasn't about to lower herself to explain.

"Fine," she snapped. "That's that. I guess we're

broken up. Have a happy Valentine's Day." Then she spun on her heel and stalked back to her seat next to Amy, who was watching her with a concerned look on her face.

Across the room, Todd watched Elizabeth plunk back down in her chair. *She looks pretty mad*, he thought gloomily.

He sighed and leaned back against the stacks so that Elizabeth couldn't glare at him. He felt really bad for making her so upset. He'd tried to handle the whole thing the right way, but it wasn't that easy. *It's better this way—she'll see that soon*, he said to console himself.

Todd straightened his shoulders and walked out of the library, trying not to look at Elizabeth as he left. Soon she would understand that they weren't quite right for each other. Sure, they had a great time hanging out together, and Todd still thought Elizabeth was one of the nicest and prettiest girls in the whole middle school. But now that he knew someone else was totally crazy about him, he felt that he had to give that someone a chance.

After all, that other girl, whoever she was, just couldn't live without him. The Valentine's card was proof of that. How could he ignore her? And even though he knew Elizabeth liked him and everything, what were her friendly feelings compared with the intense passion of the girl who wrote that letter? Todd stood up a little straighter and put his chest out as he walked down the silent, empty hall. He couldn't wait to find out who his secret admirer was.

All morning Todd had been meeting girls' eyes, looking into the face of every girl he knew, waiting for them to give him a sign. He remembered that on Friday he had been walking past his locker and there had been a group of girls standing around, talking about ice or something. Or at least they had been pretending that they were just talking. Maybe one of them had put the note in his locker. She must have asked all her friends to come along with her. Todd didn't understand why, but he knew that girls often liked to do things in little groups.

Todd ducked into the boys' room on the second floor. It would be lunchtime soon. He washed his hands at the sink and tried to smooth his hair a bit. Then he checked for zits. No major problems there. He guessed he looked all right. It was important to look his best, since he could be approached at any moment by someone who was crazy about him.

"What's the matter, Wilkins? Is your eye shadow wearing off?" Bruce Patman sneered, coming up behind him. He had just left one of the stalls and must have been there the whole time.

Todd clenched his jaw. Bruce was a seventh-grader, and he came from one of the wealthiest families in Sweet Valley. He thought he was better than anyone else in school and was always acting obnoxious and conceited.

"Maybe you're thinking about a new 'do for the dance," Bruce suggested sarcastically.

"Shut up, Patman," Todd said, drying his hands on a paper towel. "No one thinks you're funny."

"You know, I bet Elizabeth would like you with a pageboy," Bruce pretended to muse, one hand under his chin, his eyes narrowed. "A pretty girl like her deserves a pretty boyfriend, right?"

"Shove off," Todd muttered, pushing his way out of the room. He could hear Bruce's laughter behind him as the lunchtime bell rang and the students flooded the halls. Todd was swept up in the swarm and soon put Bruce out of his mind.

He stared into girls' eyes whenever he could, even girls he didn't know. He wanted to give everyone a chance. Why hadn't his secret admirer approached him yet?

Oh, of course—she knew about Elizabeth, Todd realized. She figured they already made a date for the dance and hadn't wanted to intrude.

But he had fixed that—he had gotten out of it just in time. Probably by the end of lunch everyone would know that he and Elizabeth had broken up. Todd was sure that then his secret admirer would reveal her identity.

*   *   *

Jessica sat at the sign-up table in the cafeteria, busily writing down people's orders for special cheers. The Boosters had decided to take turns either actually performing the cheers or taking orders.

"Hi, Jessica," Aaron said, coming up to the table.

Jessica gave him a big smile. *Order a cheer. Ask me to the dance,* she begged him silently. "Hi, Aaron," she said.

"How's everything going?" he asked.

"Fine, fine. Getting lots of orders," Jessica said pointedly.

Aaron smiled. "Great. Listen, I'm going to get in line. You want me to save you a place?"

Jessica couldn't believe it. Here he was at the sign-up table and he *wasn't* ordering her a cheer?

"Um, OK," she said.

"OK. See you in a few." With a little wave, Aaron dashed off to the lunch line.

Jessica tried to contain her frustration. He still had a couple days to order a cheer and ask her to the dance. *But he'd better get on it.*

Jessica watched as across the cafeteria the Boosters trooped in, waving their red-and-white pom-poms. They quickly got into formation and led off with one of today's cheers:

> "You know you are a *sweet*heart
> I really think you're *keen*
> I hate it when we're *a*-part

Julie *Por*ter, don't be mean!
Be my Valentine! Yay!"

The Boosters jumped up in high kicks, shaking their pom-poms. At her lunch table in the middle of the room, Julie Porter sat up, a shocked expression on her face. She whirled around to stare at the Boosters.

"Me?" she squeaked. "Whose sweetheart am I?"

Janet Howell stepped forward and unrolled Julie's cheer order. "With love from—Anonymous!" she read.

Julie blushed prettily as the whole cafeteria erupted into calls and applause.

Jessica was laughing over at the sign-up table. "That was a great cheer," she said as Winston joined her for his shift at the order table. "I can't believe Ellen Riteman came up with something so cute."

"I know someone else who came up with something cute," Winston said grimly, dropping his bagged lunch on the table.

"Who?" Jessica said eagerly.

"Todd Wilkins," Winston said, opening his lunch. "He just broke up with Elizabeth."

Jessica felt her mouth drop open. She looked around the cafeteria and spotted Todd, standing in the lunch line. He was talking to Ken Matthews, but his eyes were roaming the room like moths flitting around a floodlight. What was his problem?

"That's really incredible," Jessica said, both shocked and angry. "It's four days until Valentine's Day, and he breaks up with her *now*?"

Winston nodded, taking a bite of his sandwich. "Yeah. Really tacky," he agreed. "And from what I heard, it was for no good reason, either. He just wants to see other people."

"Other people?" Jessica snorted. "Who else would go out with boring Todd Wilkins except my poor deluded sister?" She searched the cafeteria for Elizabeth. There she was, sitting with Amy and Maria. She looked pretty OK—maybe just a little bit down. Jessica made up her mind to try to do something nice for Elizabeth after school.

Hmm, what could I do that would make Elizabeth feel better? Jessica wondered. Maybe she could take Elizabeth's turn setting the table. Elizabeth would be shocked.

Just then Jessica saw Aaron walk up to Elizabeth's table and sit down next to her. He leaned over and whispered something in her ear. Elizabeth smiled.

Jessica frowned. *What's he doing? What do they have to whisper about?* She felt her chest tighten. Aaron couldn't be thinking about asking *Elizabeth* to the dance, could he?

As Elizabeth smiled and nodded at Aaron, Scott Joslin slid his tray onto the table across from

Elizabeth. She looked surprised. He said something to her, and she laughed.

Jessica breathed a sigh of relief. They were just being nice to her because they'd heard about her and Todd. Or at least Aaron was just being nice—maybe Scott was trying to ask her out. *Ha!* Jessica thought. *I hope Todd is getting an eyeful of this. That'll teach him to dump my sister four days before Valentine's Day. She's much too good for him anyway. Jerk.*

Seven

"Wow! Some of these lovegrams are really—romantic," Mr. Bowman declared on Monday afternoon. He was sitting at his desk in the *Sixers* office, reading the previous Friday's issue of the sixth-grade newspaper.

"You think so?" Elizabeth couldn't help feeling pleased, since she had written quite a few of them. "I think it's great that so many people are baring their innermost feelings for Valentine's Day." *Except Todd, of course. I could have lived without him baring his innermost feelings.*

"Yes, I think some of these are . . . *remarkably* romantic," Mr. Bowman said.

Elizabeth nodded. She was proud of herself for the way she was holding her head up, even during the Todd disaster. Her own romance was crumbling into dust, but she was still glad that she could help others.

"I guess romance is really in the air," Elizabeth remarked.

"I had no idea that these lovegrams were going to be quite so . . ." Mr. Bowman seemed to be searching for the right word.

"Passionate?" Elizabeth suggested.

"Yes! Passionate," Mr. Bowman agreed. "It's almost . . . shocking."

Grinning, Elizabeth slung her backpack over one shoulder. This was great. Even Mr. Bowman was bowled over by her poems. *Maybe I shouldn't be a journalist after all,* she mused as she waved goodbye and headed out the door. Maybe she would just write poetry, books and books of romantic love poetry, when she grew up. It was something she had never considered before. Journalism had always seemed the most interesting thing to do. But this year, with so much Valentine's activity going on, she felt much more inclined to romance. *Of course, it would help if I actually had a romance going myself,* she thought a little glumly.

As she headed down the hall, Elizabeth pictured herself living alone in some little cottage somewhere. It had a white picket fence and a climbing rose reaching up one wall. Inside, in a small, feminine, light-filled study, Elizabeth saw herself writing her romantic poetry. A large, furry cat sat at her feet, washing its paw. Various awards and glowing book reviews were framed on the walls.

That's me, Elizabeth thought somewhat sadly. *I'll just be an old maid with a cat, writing my love poems to no one. Everyone will think I'm the most romantic woman alive, but they won't know that I'm a complete failure at relationships. It will be my secret.*

Good grief, I thought the school day would never end, Lila grumbled to herself. She was in her bedroom, digging in her drawer for her new bathing suit as soon as she got home from school on Monday. It had been a really rough day. First thing this morning, her dad had found the sales slip for her new outfit and had hit the roof. He'd demanded that she take it back, and she'd refused. In the end, she'd won, but she hated arguing with her father.

Then there had been seven tortured hours of school, filled with constant pestering from the Unicorns.

"What is Gray going to wear? Where will you eat first? Is he going to bring flowers? Does he have a friend?" Lila mimicked as she squirmed into her suit. Everything was Gray this and Gray that. It seemed as though a hundred-pound weight were dangling right over her head, just waiting to drop down on her.

There's only one thing to do, she thought as she grabbed a large, fluffy beach towel and stomped downstairs. *I have to find a real date, and soon. Then I can kill Gray off gracefully.* Obviously, the breaking-up-with-Gray-and-going-to-the-dance-alone plan wasn't working—every time one of the Unicorns got all impressed and jealous over her dream date, she just *had* to tell them more about the mythical Gray. It was irresistible. And now her only choice was to find a Gray substitute—someone even more perfect and impressive.

Great, she thought, rolling her eyes. *I'll just happen to meet someone who's gorgeous and romantic and sweet and adoring. No prob. Happens all the time.*

Lila groaned silently. How did she manage to get into such a huge mess in the first place? Jessica's annoying question replayed in her head. *So why did you break up with him?* Lila wished Jessica had just minded her own business.

Lila stomped into the kitchen and looked for her after-school snack, then remembered it was Mrs. Pervis's day off. She would have to get her own snack. *Like I really need this today,* she thought gloomily.

Just as she was loading a tray with a can of soda, some cookies, and an apple, the phone rang. Lila made a face as she recognized Jessica's cheerful voice.

"It's gorgeous outside—want to go do something?" Jessica suggested. "We could ride our bikes to the mall."

"No, thanks," Lila said abruptly. "I'm just going to hang out here." *Alone.*

"By yourself? Or is Gray coming over?" Jessica asked.

There she goes again—not minding her own business, Lila thought testily. "Well, Gray might come over," she said casually, unable to control herself.

As Jessica was digesting this, the call-waiting beeped. "Hang on," Lila instructed. She pushed the button. "Hello?"

"Lila? Hi, sweetie," said her father.

"Hey, Dad. I'm on the other line," Lila said.

"This won't take a minute. It's Mrs. Pervis's day off, so I thought we'd grill steaks tonight, OK? Could you please take those T-bones out of the freezer now so they'll be ready? Thanks. See you soon."

Click. Lila pressed the button again.

"Lila?" Jessica said eagerly. "Was that Gray on the phone?"

"Uh-huh," Lila answered before she could stop herself. "Just checking on some details for the dance." *That does it. I'm definitely losing my mind,* she thought.

"He's so romantic," Jessica said. Lila thought she could detect a note of sadness in her voice. "You're lucky to have a boyfriend like that. All I have is Aaron, and he still hasn't asked me to the dance."

"Oh, I'm sure he will, Jess," Lila said briskly. "Aaron's a nice guy. I mean, he's not Gray, of course, but he's not a total slime like Todd."

"Yeah." Jessica sounded unconvinced. "Can you believe he did that? Which reminds me—I have to go set the table for Elizabeth. I guess I'll talk to you later."

"OK. I better go, too. Gray's coming over soon," Lila said before hanging up the phone.

I'm totally and completely nuts, Lila thought as she walked across the lawn to the pool, holding her snack tray. *This whole Gray business is going to drive me—*

"Aieeeee!" The next thing Lila knew, she was flat on her stomach on the grass. The tray had flown out of her hands and skittered across the lawn several feet away. The cookies were strewn over the grass, and the apple had rolled under a bush.

"Wha—?" she gasped. Then she slowly pulled herself up.

"Oh, gosh, are you OK?" A boy in old, raggedy clothes ran up to her and grabbed her hand. Lila snatched it back, glaring at him suspiciously. He was sweaty and had dirt streaks across his forehead.

"Get off me, you twit," she snapped. "What are you doing here, anyway? This is a private estate."

She scrambled to her feet, brushing herself off.

The boy looked down at her—he was several inches taller than she was. "I'm Justin Pratt," he said with a smile, holding out his hand, which was covered with dirt, too. "Mr. Pratt's grandson. I'm helping out with the garden after school until Grandpa's back is better."

Narrowing her eyes, Lila glared at his hand. He sheepishly pulled it back and stuck it in the pocket of his dirty jeans. She could hardly see what he looked like—leaves were stuck in his hair, his clothes were covered with bits of earth and grass.

"I was just digging up the south bed," Justin explained self-consciously. "I finished raking a little while ago." His eyes strayed guiltily to her feet.

Lila looked down, and her face contorted with rage. A rake! She had tripped on a rake! This dolt must have left it lying right in her path. This was turning out to be the worst day ever!

"You idiot!" she cried, pointing down at the rake. "I could have killed myself! How dare you leave a dangerous object around like this? Do you know who I am? I'm Lila Fowler! Do you know what would have happened to you if I had *died* by tripping on this rake? My dad would have killed you. He'd probably stick your head on a post, right in the middle of the lawn, for everyone to see!"

"Uh, um," the boy stammered, his green eyes wide. Nervously he pushed a dirt-covered hand through his thick, slightly wavy dark-chestnut hair. "Gosh, Lila . . . Ms. Fowler," he quickly amended. "I didn't mean to . . ." After looking around nervously, he dropped to his knees and started gathering cookies.

"Didn't mean to!" Lila screeched, stamping her foot.

Blowing bits of stray grass off the cookies, Justin put them back on the plate and set the plate on the tray.

Lila watched him in furious disbelief. Did he think she was interested in cookies that had rolled all over the ground?

"Forget the cookies!" she cried, stamping her foot again. Justin jumped and then froze, holding one cookie in his hand. Lila glared at him. "Just get the soda under the lounge chair," she hissed through clenched teeth. Tapping her foot, she waited impatiently while he scrambled beneath the chair, retrieved her can of soda, and brushed it off. Then, standing up, he shyly held the cold can out to her.

Without a word, Lila snatched it out of his hand and stalked to the other end of the pool. Once there, she put the soda on a table, shrugged off her wrap, and dove headfirst into the pool's warm blue water. *Old Mr. Pratt better get well soon,* she thought as she angrily began doing laps. *If I have to put up with his dolt of a grandson much longer, I'm going to have them* both *fired.*

*   *   *

Leaning on the rake, Justin watched as Lila churned up little waves. She finished one lap and started another, her face set in angry determination. *What a girl*, he thought, still feeling somewhat stunned by their encounter. In his eighth-grade class at Lovett Academy, which he attended on scholarship, Justin knew lots of girls. But this girl was gorgeous. Sure, she had a temper, but that was what gave her her spark, her fire, her spirit. Compared with her, most of the girls he was friends with seemed kind of wimpy. But Lila obviously had guts, the way she had fearlessly lit into him like that. *Lila with the flashing eyes*, he thought dreamily, watching her for a few moments more before gathering up his tools and heading off for the perennial border by the side of the house. *Why didn't Grandpa tell me about her? Surely this couldn't be the "obnoxious snip of a girl" he warned me about. This girl's fantastic.* He took one last, long glance at her. She had just surfaced in the pool and flung her long, wet brown hair back like a whip. Floating on her back, she spat a stream of water into the air.

Gosh, she's fantastic, Justin thought, shaking his head. Then he hitched up his jeans and went back to work.

Brrng. Brrrng.

"I got it!" Steven yelled, flying for the phone in the family room on Monday night. He tackled it and swept it to the ground just seconds ahead of Jessica. "Get off!" he ordered as Jessica toppled on top of him.

Giggling, Jessica slid over onto the floor. Elizabeth barely looked up from where she was reading a magazine on the couch. Jessica and Steven had been fighting over the phone all night.

"Hello?" Steven said hopefully into the phone. Instantly, his forehead creased and his brows came together. "Oh. Yeah, I guess so. Hang on."

Don't let it be for me, Elizabeth thought, watching Steven out of the corner of her eye. Ever since people had started finding out about her and Todd, guys had been calling her up. Some of them just wanted to offer friendly support. But more than one guy had wanted to ask her to the dance. It was starting to make her feel weird.

"Elizabeth, some geek wants you," Steven said, putting his hand over the receiver. Then he dropped the phone onto the floor with a clatter, got to his feet, and walked away.

Jessica leaned against the family room sofa, looking disappointed. Elizabeth couldn't blame her. She knew Jessica was waiting for Aaron to call. Elizabeth wished he would. But so far every time the phone had rung tonight, it had been for Elizabeth.

"Hello?" she said, picking up the phone.

"Hey, Elizabeth, it's Bruce."

Elizabeth's eyes widened, and she frantically beckoned Jessica over to listen.

Scooting closer, Jessica put her head against Elizabeth's so she could hear.

"Yeah, so, you know, I heard Wilkins cut you loose," Bruce said casually to Elizabeth. "I'm figuring you need a date for the dance. Luckily, I'm still available."

Jessica put her hand over her mouth and fell over onto the carpet, trying to stifle her giggles.

"Gee, Bruce, I don't know," Elizabeth murmured, smirking at Jessica.

"Hey, say the word, Elizabeth," Bruce said confidently. "This is your chance. Go for it."

Elizabeth rolled her eyes at Jessica. This was too much. She didn't really want to go to the dance with anyone but Todd—and especially not with Bruce Patman.

"Uh, well, I'm still not sure I'm going to go to the dance at all," Elizabeth said hesitantly. "Or maybe I'll go by myself or something. . . ." She fell silent again.

A few feet away, Jessica buried her face in a pillow and let her giggles come.

"Well, tell you what," Bruce said. "I'll give you twenty-four hours to think about it. How's that? An exclusive offer till this time tomorrow. After that, I'll have to ask some other lucky girl. Fair enough, right?"

"Um, right," Elizabeth said. "I'll think about it. Thanks, Bruce. It was nice of you to ask me." She hung up the phone with a sigh.

"Bruce Patman asked you to the dance?" Jessica shrieked, dancing around the family room with her pillow. "I can't believe it! Wait till the Unicorns hear about this!"

Elizabeth whirled to face her twin. She knew that most of the Unicorns considered Bruce a hot catch, since he was cute and rich. Things like personality weren't all that important to the Unicorns.

"Jessica! Don't you dare tell anyone about it!" she ordered. "I don't want to be teased by everyone in school."

"But Elizabeth," Jessica said in a wheedling tone, "it'll be a *good* kind of attention. The Unicorns will die when they hear that one of the most important boys in seventh grade asked you out."

"Gee, just what I've always wanted—the approval of the Unicorns," Elizabeth said.

Jessica put an arm around Elizabeth's shoulders. "But, Lizzie, just think of how upset Todd will be when he hears about it," she said in a coaxing tone. "Six hours after he dumped you, his archenemy is begging you for a date. Todd hates Bruce. It'll make him so sorry that he broke up with you."

Elizabeth grimaced. "I don't care. I want him to be upset without knowing about Bruce. Please, Jessica, promise me you won't tell."

Jessica let out a huge sigh. "Oh, all right," she said grumpily. "Just rob me of the hottest piece of gossip in who knows how long, that's all. But in my opinion, Todd deserves it."

"Maybe he does," Elizabeth said ruefully. "I ignored him all afternoon, and he didn't seem to notice. Every time I saw him he seemed to be staring at other girls. But that doesn't mean I want everyone to know about Bruce."

"OK, OK," Jessica said. "But Todd's girl watching is pretty disgusting. It's almost as disgusting as not being asked to the dance at *all* by someone you were *sure* would have asked you by now."

"I'm sure Aaron will call soon," Elizabeth comforted her.

"Well, I probably won't even know if he does, since the phone's constantly tied up with guys calling *you*."

"I'm sorry," Elizabeth said. "But it's not my fault. Do you think I *wanted* Bruce to call me?"

Jessica looked more cheerful for a second. "Lizzie, are you sure I can't just drop a hint—"

"No!" Elizabeth crossed her arms over her chest.

"I won't actually say his name—"

"No way, José!" Elizabeth said firmly.

Ten minutes later the phone rang again. Before Jessica could pounce on it in the family room, however, her mother picked it up in the kitchen.

"Hello, Aaron," Jessica heard her say.

"Yes!" Jessica punched her fist in the air and did a little victory dance in front of Elizabeth. "This is it!" Beaming, she looked at her mother as she walked into the family room.

"Elizabeth," Mrs. Wakefield said, "Aaron Dallas wants to talk to you."

Jessica raised her eyebrows in shock. "Her! What does he want to talk to *her* about?"

With a look of confusion, Elizabeth picked up the phone. "Hello?" she said, not meeting Jessica's outraged expression. "Hi, Aaron. Uh-huh. Yeah. I understand." She turned her back so Jessica couldn't see her, and Jessica quickly ran around to face her again. "No, I don't think that's a good idea," Elizabeth said, avoiding Jessica's eyes. "Yeah, that would be better. Yeah, I think so." Jessica stood right in front of Elizabeth and glared into her face. Elizabeth turned again, and Jessica felt her blood start to boil.

"OK," Elizabeth said. "Uh-huh. OK, here she is." Elizabeth turned around and finally held the phone out to Jessica. Jessica snatched it away.

"Aaron?" she said, her voice sounding strangled.

"Hi, Jessica," Aaron said, sounding exactly the way he always did. "Boy, that's some news about Todd and Elizabeth, huh? I hope he knows what he's doing. Anyway, I have something to ask you."

Jessica's heart began to flutter. All her anxiety about his talking to Elizabeth first faded. "Yes?" she asked breathlessly.

"Yeah. I was wondering if you were going to watch *Lifeguard Central* tonight."

Jessica felt her heart sink slowly into her stomach. *Lifeguard Central? What does that have to do with Valentine's Day?* "Um, yeah, probably," Jessica confirmed, her mind reeling.

"Great. Would you mind taping it for me? I have to go to my grandmother's house, and I don't want to miss it."

Jessica took the phone away from her ear and stared at it in disbelief. That was it? That was the big question? "Yeah, sure, Aaron," she said briskly. "Anything else?"

"Nope," Aaron said cheerfully. "Except . . ."

Jessica held her breath. "Yes?"

"Well, I thought you looked really pretty today," he whispered. "I liked that pink sweater."

"Thanks, Aaron," Jessica said, quickly hanging up. She looked at Elizabeth suspiciously.

"So why was Aaron calling you?" she demanded.

Elizabeth looked up from her math homework. "Um, he needed to borrow some geography notes."

"He's not in your geography class," Jessica pointed out, tapping her foot against the floor.

"No," Elizabeth agreed. "But Amy is, and he

knows we study together, so . . . anyway, did he ask you to the dance?"

"No, he didn't!" Jessica practically shouted. "Did he ask *you*?"

"Me?" Elizabeth looked startled. "Of course not. He's *your* boyfriend."

"I'm beginning to think he's hardly even my friend, much less my boyfriend," Jessica said, pacing in angry circles on the family room carpet.

"Oh, calm down, Jess," Elizabeth said. "I'm sure he's going to ask you. Don't worry about it."

"That's easy for you to say," Jessica said. "You've already turned down a million invitations!"

"More like a few," Elizabeth corrected. "And if you want, I'll let you go with Bruce. I'm sure it wouldn't matter to him which of us he goes with. We look identical, after all."

Jessica scowled at her sister. "Oh, you are *so* funny," she said with narrowed eyes. She was starting to think that Todd's breaking up with Elizabeth was the worst thing that had ever happened to *either* of them.

Eight

◇

I bet it's Brooke Dennis, Todd thought triumphantly right before lunch on Tuesday as he threw
his books in his locker. She's my secret admirer—
the girl who's so totally crazy about me. She had to
be the one. First of all, most of the girls he knew
were sort of paired up with someone already. But
not Brooke. Second, this morning he had been
standing behind Brooke at the bus stop, and she
asked to borrow fifteen cents. A girl didn't borrow
money from just anyone. She had to feel comfortable with the person. Third, right after English
class this morning, Todd had bumped into Brooke
as they were filing into the hall.

Leaning against his closed locker, Todd remembered the romantic moment.

"Oh, sorry," he had said.

"No prob," Brooke had said in response. As in, *I don't mind if you bump into me, Todd.* And bumping was sort of like hugging, wasn't it? So obviously if Brooke didn't mind Todd bumping into her, she was telling him that she wouldn't mind almost hugging him.

It was like a neon sign had lit up inside his head.

But what should he do next? He had to give her some kind of signal back. After she had taken that big chance of sending him the Valentine's card, the next step was up to him.

Taking a deep breath, Todd pushed his hair off his forehead. Why was he nervous? He already knew that Brooke was crazy about him. She would be thrilled if she knew he liked her, too.

Just then, as though she had been reading his mind, Brooke Dennis came out of the girls' locker room and headed toward the cafeteria. *She timed that one pretty perfectly,* Todd thought, chuckling to himself. *I guess we're really on the same wavelength.*

"Hey, Brooke," he called. "Wait a sec."

Brooke turned, looking surprised. "Hi, Todd. What's up?"

Like you don't know. What a kidder. Todd gave her an understanding smile. "So," he said, lowering his voice, "do you always write love notes, or am I a special case?"

Brooke's eyes widened. "Excuse me?"

Todd touched her gently on the shoulder. "Look,

Brooke, we don't have to play games. I know you like me. I won't make you say it again. Just tell me what time to pick you up for the dance."

"Play games? Tell you again?" Brooke looked bewildered.

For the first time Todd started to feel a tiny trickle of doubt creeping down his spine. It *had* been Brooke, right? It *had* to have been Brooke.

"I'm sorry, Todd," Brooke said, shrugging her shoulders. "But Jake Hamilton has already asked me to the dance."

"Jake . . ." Todd felt the ground shift beneath his feet. Desperately, he tried to think of something to say that would let him save face.

"See you later, Todd," Brooke said apologetically. "Thanks, anyway." Then she was gone.

"Later," he managed weakly. Biting his lip, he turned and headed away from the cafeteria. OK, so he had been wrong about Brooke. It was an honest mistake. The next time, he would just be doubly sure, that's all.

"What should we look at first? Shoes or earrings?" Tamara Chase asked her fellow Unicorns on Tuesday afternoon at the Valley Mall.

"Well, I don't need shoes, but I'll go look if you guys want to," Ellen Riteman volunteered.

Lila drummed her fingers against a huge planter filled with palm trees. She didn't care where they went, but this dithering back and forth was making her crazy. "I vote for shoes," she said briskly.

"Jessica?" Janet Howell prompted.

Jessica sighed. "It doesn't matter," she said despondently.

"Good, shoes it is." Lila set off toward the Wild Pair, one of her favorite shoe stores at the mall. Jessica soon caught up with her, and Lila shot her a glance. "Still no word from Aaron, huh?" Lila asked.

"No." Jessica looked incredibly depressed. Lila didn't know whose situation was worse: Jessica had a boyfriend who hadn't asked her to the dance but probably would, unless he pulled a Todd; Lila had no boyfriend at all, but he'd already asked her to the dance. The whole thing was giving her a headache. She couldn't quite forget that the whole Gray business was all Jessica's fault, too.

Lila headed into the Wild Pair and quickly selected three different black shoes, any of which would probably work with her outfit. She plopped down in a chair and started trying them on.

"Ohh, cute," Janet said approvingly, looking at the black suede platform shoes Lila was trying on. "Those would look great with your bell-bottoms. And they'd be easy to dance in, too."

Lila looked down, but couldn't work up much enthusiasm. "Yeah, they're OK."

"Have I told you what band we hired for the

dance?" Janet continued. This year the eighth-graders had taken care of the music, the seventh-graders were in charge of the decorations, and the sixth-graders were doing the food.

Lila shook her head.

"Walled Temple!" Janet's eyes sparkled. "They're a really great band. They played at Sweet Valley High for their Christmas prom."

"Oh. Neat," Lila said.

Ellen came to sit next to Lila. "We'll have to make sure they play lots of slow songs, right, Lila?" She smirked. "So you and Gray will have plenty of time together."

Tamara walked in front of them like a model, showing off a pair of low heels. "Is Gray tall, or do you have to wear flats when you see him?" she asked.

Lila looked down at her black leather mules. "No, he's really tall," she said without thinking. It was becoming so easy to lie. "I can wear anything I want. In fact, he likes it when I wear shoes with heels."

"Wow," Ellen said, wiggling her eyebrows. "It's pretty serious when a guy actually notices what you wear."

Lila flipped her hair back. "Gray always notices what I wear," she said proudly. "Just yesterday he said he liked my cinnamon sweater."

Janet looked at Lila appraisingly. "Well, I think

we'll all have fabulous dates to the Valentine's dance. Right, Tamara?"

"Right," Tamara agreed. "Janet, come look at these other shoes. . . ."

As they walked away, Lila sat in her chair, staring down at the three pairs she had tried on.

"They're all nice," Jessica said morosely, sitting down next to her. She dropped her head into her hands and looked at her own sneakered feet.

"So which ones are you getting?" Ellen asked. "I liked the platforms."

"Oh, I can't decide," Lila said. "I better just take all three, try them on at home, and then bring two back."

"Good idea. And, um, Lila?" Ellen asked, hesitating. "Have you had a chance to talk to Gray?"

"About what?" Lila said, turning her foot sideways and looking at the shoe.

"About, you know. If he has a friend for me for the Valentine's dance."

"Um . . ." Lila stalled. If she said no, she hadn't asked him, then she'd look like a bad friend. If she said no, Gray didn't have a friend, then it might seem that he hadn't put any effort into it and wasn't such a great guy after all.

Lila took a deep breath. "Uh, yeah, I mentioned it to him," she said slowly. "And, um, he said he'd ask around. He's going to ask around, and let us know tomorrow or the next day. But he said that

Lovett's having their own Valentine's dance, and it's kind of late notice, so it might be best if you plan on going with a girlfriend or something."

Ellen sighed. "Yeah, probably. But I'll keep my fingers crossed. Tell Gray thanks for asking around, OK?" Standing up, she patted Lila's shoulder. "You're the best, Li."

Lila smiled weakly. *Yeah, that's me. Vote me Miss Good Citizen of the Year.*

As she put her three pairs of shoes on her credit card, Lila realized that she'd have to start putting Plan B into effect *soon*. She needed a real, flesh-and-blood reason to get rid of Gray. Namely, another guy.

I have to get a date, I have to get a date, Lila chanted to herself. She and her friends were on line at Spuds 'n' Stuffin' in the food court, taking a break from shopping. *I have to get a date,* Lila chanted again. But how?

Lila sighed and glanced around the food court. Naturally, the line next to hers was moving faster. Ellen was already ordering. It always happened that way.

Suddenly, Lila's eyes fell on the person behind Ellen. It was a guy, maybe her age, maybe a year older, and he was looking right at her and smiling. Lila's heart thumped a beat. He was really cute, with curly dark-blond hair and brown eyes.

Smiling back, Lila flipped her hair over her shoulder flirtatiously, and kept her eyes on him as they both moved forward in line. *He's adorable*, she thought excitedly. *This could be the answer to all my problems.* If she could somehow get this cute guy to take her to the dance on Friday, everything would be wonderful again. She'd just tell her friends that she and Gray had broken up over Gray's jealousy. *And he definitely has a good reason to be jealous*, Lila thought, looking again at her cute blond stranger.

As Lila ordered some curly fries, the cute boy headed over to his table with one last look at her. Lila winked at him, and he gave her a big smile. She decided to make some excuse to go over to his table, just as the Unicorns were leaving, and slip him her phone number. He would probably call tonight, and by bedtime all her troubles would be over.

Happily, Lila sat down and dug into her fries. She was starving. For the first time in days, she didn't have a nervous stomachache.

"Excuse me," someone with a nice, deep voice said from over her shoulder.

Lila looked up and tried to control her breathing. It was the cute guy. Her Valentine's date. Her lifesaver.

"I hope you don't mind, but I couldn't help noticing you," he told her with a smile, looking deeply into her eyes.

Lila stared at him, aware that all the Unicorns were silent with amazement. *This is so perfect, so romantic . . .*

"I was wondering, I mean, I know this is short notice, and we don't really know each other, but do you think maybe this Friday night—"

Yes! Yes, yes, yes!

"Take a hike, bucko," Jessica said firmly, waving a fry in the air. "Lila has a date for Friday. In fact, she has a date every Friday, because she has a fabulous boyfriend. *Comprende?*"

Lila's heart sank. *Why can't you just stay out of it, Jessica?* She shot a glare at her ex–best friend.

"That's right," Janet jumped in. "Her boyfriend's name is Gray, and you better not let him catch you asking her out."

The adorable boy frowned and looked at Lila in confusion. Lila met his eyes, mutely begging him not to listen to her incredibly stupid friends.

"Well, sorry," he said, looking irritated. "I guess I got the wrong message." Then he turned and stomped back over to his table.

No, no, you didn't, you didn't get the wrong message at all, please, please, come back. Lila felt like crying into her curly fries.

"Whew!" Jessica said cheerfully, munching on a fry. "Close call, huh? Good thing Gray won't find out about that guy. Right, Li?"

Jessica Wakefield, your days are numbered. Lila

couldn't help glaring at her, and Jessica stopped in mid-fry.

"What?" she demanded. "Why are you looking at me that way?"

"Gosh, Lila," Tamara said disapprovingly. "You can't have *all* the cute guys, you know. I mean, leave some for the rest of us."

"Yeah," Janet agreed. "When you have someone as fabulous as Gray, it's not like you need to have a backup guy or anything."

Lila bit her lip and cleared her throat. "A *backup* guy? Oh, that's really too funny. Ha, ha, ha, ha. After all, Gray's *more* than enough for any girl. It's just that I wanted to let that poor boy down a little more gently, that's all."

Janet raised her eyebrows. "This is so unlike you, Lila. I guess love really does make a person kinder."

"Yeah, I guess it does," Lila agreed.

Nine

◇

"Are you sure it'll be OK?" Melissa McCormick asked Elizabeth nervously, playing with a piece of her hair. It was Wednesday morning before school, and Elizabeth was sitting at the *Sixers* table in the cafeteria, composing lovegrams.

Elizabeth gave Melissa a reassuring smile. "I'm sure. Trust me, he'll love it."

"It just sounds so . . . so—"

"Romantic? It's supposed to. It's Valentine's Day, remember?" Elizabeth said teasingly. "Now, quit worrying about it." Elizabeth folded up Melissa's order form and slipped it into a folder. "That'll be two fifty, please."

Silently, Melissa paid her money, then turned and headed for the door. She looked back a couple of times, biting her lip.

Elizabeth gave her a friendly smile and a wave. Maybe her own love life was in the pits, but she felt good about helping other people. Smiling to herself, she straightened up her order forms and got ready for her next customer.

Good, I look awful, Lila thought as she checked her appearance in her hand mirror. She was sitting in the backseat of her father's limousine before school on Wednesday morning, and she was about to carry out plan C—the horrible, dreadful breakup-with-Gray plan.

This morning she had carefully put a little blush on her nose, and pale powder everywhere else. Now, taking a bag out of her purse, she opened it and inhaled deeply. Instantly, her eyes began watering, her nose began running, and she sneezed. She sealed the bag and stuffed it back in her purse, hoping no one would smell the onion.

Then she took a deep breath, squared her shoulders, and got out of the car. Several Unicorns were already walking toward her, having spotted the limo.

"Lila!" Jessica exclaimed. "What's the matter? You look terrible."

Janet, Ellen, and Kimberly Haver crowded around her.

Lila looked down, trying to appear miserable. "Gray and I broke up last night," she whimpered, hunching her shoulders.

Janet gasped. "What? Oh, no. Poor Lila. And only two days before the dance."

"That's terrible," Kimberly agreed, looking concerned. "What are you going to do?"

"I guess I'll just go to the dance alone," Lila choked out, sniffling into a Kleenex.

"But I don't understand," Jessica said. "Why did you guys break up? You two were made for each other."

Lila looked at Jessica, whose open, concerned face was right in front of her. In all her determination to look brokenhearted, Lila had forgotten to come up with a reason. "Uh," she stammered, "I, uh . . . forgot his birthday yesterday. Now he thinks I don't care. It was so stupid of me!" She looked down sadly again as they headed into school.

"Oh, no, how could he think you don't care?" Ellen asked. "Doesn't he know you're crazy about him? This is terrible."

"I know, I know," Lila agreed. "He told me days ago about his birthday, but I've had so many things on my mind. I was hoping I could make it up to him on Valentine's Day, but he says it's all over." She shook her head miserably.

"Oh, Lila." Janet tried to soothe her as they headed toward their homeroom. "What a shame. Now you won't have a date for the dance."

Lila gritted her teeth. "Yeah, I guess so. How embarrassing." She hunched over and shuffled her feet sadly down the corridor. She once thought that showing up at the dance alone would be the worst humiliation in the world, but now she didn't care how embarrassed she was at the dance. Not after what Gray had put her through this week.

OK. This time I'm really sure. It's gotta be her, Todd thought, looking around his sixth-period science class. There she was: Maria Slater. She'd always been really friendly to him, and today she'd given him a big smile when he came into the science lab. And when they had been taking equipment out of the supply closet for their experiments, she had pulled down a Bunsen burner for him.

How much more obvious could a girl be?

He remembered other things in the past, other signals she had been sending him. Sitting next to Elizabeth at lunch, *when Todd was there*. Being at Elizabeth's house, *when Todd called*. Now he saw that she'd been keeping her feelings for him hidden—after all, she was a good friend of Elizabeth's. Maria had probably been struggling with her feelings for Todd for a long time.

Todd smiled to himself. As far as secret admirers went, Maria was a great catch. She was really pretty, and she even used to be a famous movie star. How many guys could say that about their secret admirer?

Suddenly, Todd flushed, thinking about the mistake he'd made about Brooke Dennis yesterday. It had been really embarrassing, especially when the Boosters had performed that stupid cheer that Jake had ordered for Brooke. Todd saw now that Brooke really hadn't given him that much to go on. But with Maria, it was completely different.

Frowning, he thought of how Maria and Elizabeth had always been good friends. He hoped this wouldn't ruin their friendship. Then he shook his head. They would have to work it out between themselves. He couldn't let himself get all caught up in it. He just hoped that Elizabeth wouldn't decide to fight for him.

"OK, class," Mr. Siegel called. "Everyone make sure the area around your Bunsen burner is clear. We don't want any fires."

Todd and his science lab partner, Randy Mason, set up their burner.

"Oh, boy," Randy said under his breath. "This is so exciting. Today we get to measure Fahrenheit temperatures versus Celsius." He rolled his eyes, and Todd grinned.

"Yeah," Todd muttered, opening his notebook. "Like anyone could care less."

So how can I approach Maria? he wondered as Randy poured a liquid into a small flask. He felt a little weird about it. He wished she had just sent him another note, or maybe a lovegram, suggesting where they should meet. But she hadn't. Maybe she wanted him to come to *her*. Some girls liked the guy to do all the asking. Thank heavens Elizabeth hadn't been that way. Not that it mattered anymore, of course, since things with Elizabeth were over.

"Whoa! Watch out!" Randy said, pushing Todd away from the burner. "You almost set your eyebrows on fire!"

Todd jumped back.

"OK, write down that liquid A reached 112 degrees Fahrenheit after two point one minutes," Randy instructed.

I guess I'll just have to take matters into my own hands, Todd thought as he took notes. Randy started preparing another small flask, and Todd used his asbestos pad to move the other one out of the way. *After all, the dance is just two days away.* They would need to decide when he was picking her up and if she expected flowers—all the usual girl-type details.

"OK, Todd," Randy said. "You measure the temperature of liquid B, and convert it to Celsius. I'm going to go get another flask." Randy dashed off toward the supply cabinet.

She's probably really starting to wonder when I'm going to ask her, Todd thought as he measured the temperature and did the calculation to make it a Celsius number. *I bet she's having a really hard time concentrating on this experiment with me in the room.*

Finally Todd clapped a lid on his Bunsen burner and went over one aisle to where Maria was measuring the temperature of a boiling liquid.

"Hey, Maria," he said, watching her write down some figures. He noticed that they weren't the figures he had just gotten in his experiment, but maybe she was doing it wrong. She was probably really distracted.

Maria looked up and smiled, her eyes crinkling behind her safety goggles. *Only Maria could look cute in safety goggles,* Todd thought.

"Hey, Todd," she said.

Todd waited a few moments, looking at her expectantly for signs of joy and relief that he had approached her. But instead, she was looking back at him, waiting for him to continue. *OK. She probably wants some kind of sign before she blurts out all her feelings.*

"So . . ." Todd said. "I just wanted to tell you that . . . I feel the same way." He gave her an encouraging smile.

A little crease formed between her eyebrows. "The same way?"

Wow, she's really *shy,* Todd thought. He'd never thought of Maria as shy, but obviously she was, deep down. On the other hand, she had written him that incredible love poem, which meant she was really bold, in some ways. So she was both bold and shy, which Todd thought was a totally irresistible combination.

Todd plunged ahead. "You know, the note," he continued in a low voice. "I just wanted to say, you know, if you want to go to the dance with me, that's cool."

Maria looked at him blankly, then took off her safety goggles. "Gosh, Todd, that's nice of you, but I already have a date for the dance. It's only two days away, after all."

Todd was dumbfounded. "Oh, yeah, OK," he muttered finally. "Of course, you already have a date. The dance is only two days away."

He slunk back to his desk. *Great*, he thought. *Wrong again*. He was really batting a thousand. He was starting to wish he had never gotten that stupid Valentine's poem.

Todd stared at his Bunsen burner. He decided he'd better run his temperature experiment one more time. Just in case.

It's about time, Lila thought that afternoon when the final bell rang. All she wanted was to go home and flop on her bed and celebrate her freedom from Gray. Or maybe she would go swimming and lie in the sun. Except she didn't feel like running into Jason or Jared or whatever his name was again. It seemed that anytime she was out in her yard, she would look up and there he would be, staring at her. It was creepy. Obviously, he needed to get a life.

Bundling up her books, she remembered to slouch and look unhappy as she headed for the exit door. She knew all her friends felt sorry for her—at lunchtime they hadn't even made her perform a cheer or take orders at the sign-up table. Instead she had sat alone, contentedly reading a fashion magazine as she ate. It had been the best lunch she'd had in a week. *Thank heavens Gray is dead*, she thought for the thousandth time that day. He had been by far the most annoying guy she had ever known.

As she walked out of the school building, Lila spotted Janet, Jessica, Ellen, Mandy, Kimberly, and Tamara huddled together by the side exit. Looking around carefully, Tamara held open a large bag while Janet carefully pushed a flat, white box inside. *What are they up to?* Lila thought suspiciously. If this was official Unicorn business, why hadn't she been told about it? Setting her jaw firmly, she strolled over to them.

"Hi, guys," she called.

Tamara gave a little scream, and Janet whirled around, a guilty look on her face. Jessica, Mandy, and Ellen threw their bodies in front of the box, trying to keep Lila from seeing it.

"Hey, what's going on?" Lila demanded.

"Nothing!" Janet said quickly.

Lila's eyes narrowed. "What are you doing with that box?" Peering past Jessica's shoulder, Lila tried to read the lettering on the side of the box.

"Box?" Kimberly repeated. "Oh, you mean this box here? Oh, nothing very interesting. Really."

Lila crossed her arms. "Guys, I've had a very hard day," she said, reminding them all of her heartbreak. "Now I find that my best friends have all turned against me. I can't believe this. It's almost too much to bear." She let her lower lip quiver a bit.

"Lila, we're not turning against you," Jessica protested.

"What are you doing, then?"

Mandy looked at her sheepishly and sighed. "It's . . . it's a birthday cake. For Gray," she explained. "We all felt so bad about you two breaking up. And we know how you feel about showing up at the dance without a date."

"You know, being a dateless Unicorn and everything," Kimberly added.

"The Unicorns *do* have an image to maintain," Janet reminded her gently.

"So we just thought that we'd go over to Lovett Academy and give Gray this cake," Mandy finished.

Lila stared, her mouth open.

"And tell him it was all your idea," Tamara put in.

"And beg him to reconsider," Ellen said proudly.

"After all," Janet said. "We, more than anyone, know how much Gray means to you. We can convince him you didn't mean to forget his birthday. I'm sure he'd take you to the dance then."

"No!" Lila cried, picturing in horror what would happen when her friends got to Lovett Academy and discovered there was no Gray Williams.

"Why not?" Jessica asked. "It's a great plan. And we got a really nice cake with 'Happy Birthday, dear Gray' written on it. I'm sure he'll go for it."

"Don't you want to see all the non-Unicorn girls drooling over Gray at the dance?" Janet added.

"No—I mean, yes—I mean it's not that," Lila said desperately, trying to think fast. "It's that . . . I mean, that's a really great idea, and I appreciate it, but . . . well, what I mean is, we already made up. So even though that cake is really nice and all, he's not mad anymore, so he, uh, doesn't need it. So in other words, let's just go to my house and eat it ourselves," she finished quickly. *Why doesn't the ground just open up right now and swallow me forever?*

The Unicorns stared at her.

"You made up?" Janet repeated.

"He forgave you?" Kimberly asked.

"You guys are back together?" Ellen said.

"Yes, yes, and yes," Lila repeated firmly. She took hold of the bag and tugged it gently. "Now, let's go to my house. We can watch videos and eat this fabulous cake."

"Wow, that's really great," Mandy said happily. "I was hoping you two lovebirds would make up. I knew Gray was too great a guy just to let you go like that."

"Well, OK, if you're sure," Janet said, a bemused look on her face. "Let's go to your house and eat Gray's cake."

"Great!" Lila said, leading them down the sidewalk.

Jessica fell into step beside her. "Don't get me wrong—I'm glad you and Gray made up," she said. "But I have to admit, I was kind of hoping you'd keep me company at the dance, since it looks like I won't have a date." She shuddered. "It's so embarrassing. I mean, I'm Jessica Wakefield." She let out a deep sigh.

Lila suppressed a grin. Sometimes Jessica was so full of herself. "Don't worry about it, Jessica," Lila said magnanimously. "It's really not the worst thing in the world not to have a date on Valentine's Day. Even at a totally romantic Valentine's dance. Even for a Unicorn."

Jessica glanced at her, looking slightly bitter. "That's easy for you to say. You have Gray falling all over you."

Lila couldn't help feeling a little smug. Gray *was* pretty devoted. Especially for someone who didn't even exist.

"Anyway, I don't know what to think about Aaron," Jessica said, shaking her head sadly. "I guess I'll just go to the dance with Elizabeth." She sighed again. "Oh, by the way," she said more brightly, "how did you and Gray make up? You've been at school all day." She turned expectant eyes on Lila.

The other Unicorns slowly came to a halt and looked at Lila, too.

Lila's mind froze. *How did we . . . how did we . . . darn it, Jessica! Can't you keep your big mouth shut for once?* "He, uh . . ." she began. *Dad always says a Fowler has to be able to think on her feet,* Lila remembered. "He . . . called me here at school and had me paged. During seventh period," she lied. "Didn't you hear me get called to the office?" *Brilliant, Lila, utterly brilliant.*

Lila felt pretty lucky that in fact she *had* gotten called to the office during seventh period. Her father had called to let her know that he had to go out of town unexpectedly and that he'd be back by Friday with a surprise for her.

Lila had never seen the Unicorns look so impressed and envious.

"Oh, my gosh, that was Gray?" Tamara squealed.

Lila smiled modestly.

"He had you paged at school?" Janet breathed.

Lila shrugged and looked at the ground.

"He is sooo romantic," Jessica moaned. "He's perfect."

Lila nodded and examined her fingernails.

"I need a piece of cake, quick," Mandy said.

"Let's go," Lila said cheerfully, leading the way to her house. Right at this very minute, with all the Unicorns staring at her with their tongues hanging out, she was sort of having fun. Sort of.

"Well, bye, you guys!" Lila called two hours later as her friends drifted down her gravel driveway. "Thanks again for the cake! It was really delicious."

"Bye, Lila!" Jessica called back to her.

"Congrats on getting back with Gray!" Tamara added, waving as the Unicorns disappeared down the sidewalk.

My life has really turned to mud, Lila thought, slumping against a huge white column in front of her house. What was she going to do now? She couldn't think of anything that would get her out of this mess or anything that would cheer her up.

A slight rustling of a nearby bush caught her eye. She looked up to see that annoying green-eyed Jasper person, staring at her over the hedge.

"What do *you* want?" she snapped, angry that he had seen her looking depressed.

"Nothing, Ms. Fowler," he replied in a respectful tone of voice.

Her eyes narrowed angrily, she turned and stomped back into the house, slamming the door behind her. *Peasant*, she thought. He had some nerve.

Ten

◇

"Oh, Todd, hang on a minute," Caroline Pearce called just as Todd left the school building and was walking across the playing field.

Todd shifted his backpack and turned around. It was only ten o'clock in the morning, and he'd already had a bad day. Just last period he had totally flunked a history test. Usually, he and Elizabeth studied together. But this week they hadn't even been talking, and he hadn't been able to concentrate on his schoolwork.

Caroline flipped back her long red French braid and smiled at him. "Just the person I've been looking for. I've been trying to get a hold of you all week."

"What's up, Caroline?" Todd asked in a bored tone. Then a chill crept up the back of his neck.

She'd been looking for him all week? *Oh, no,* he thought. *Please, please, no.* His secret admirer *couldn't* be Caroline Pearce! Caroline was the biggest gossip in sixth grade and really annoying.

"I wanted to know if it's true that you and Elizabeth really broke up," Caroline said, her green eyes locked on his.

"Well, uh, yeah, I guess so," Todd said carefully.

"And that you're not going to the dance with anyone else?" she pressed.

Todd took a deep breath. "Um, not yet. I might not go at all. Yeah, I think that's probably the best idea. I won't go at all. Probably I'll just stay home."

"Have you talked to Elizabeth lately?" Caroline asked.

What is she trying to get at? Todd wondered. *I feel like she's interviewing me or something.*

"No, not really," he said abruptly.

"So you don't know whether she's going to the dance with Bruce Patman or not?" Caroline asked eagerly.

Todd stared at her. "What? Why would she go with Bruce?"

"Because Bruce asked her, that's why," Caroline said smugly.

"Bruce asked Elizabeth . . ." Todd clenched his fists. That jerk! "There's no way she would go with Bruce," he said tightly.

"How do you know?" Caroline asked. "If you

haven't talked to her . . . maybe she is."

"I don't need to talk to her," Todd said through clenched teeth. "I know Elizabeth, and I know she would never go out with that stuck-up jerk."

Caroline looked impatient. "Well, obviously you don't know *anything*. Later, Todd." Turning, she flounced away.

Todd stared after her. *Well, at least it doesn't seem like she's my secret admirer,* he consoled himself. *The only thing she wants from me is gossip.*

He walked down the hall, dragging his feet. He couldn't get Caroline's words out of his mind. *I can't believe that stupid Bruce Patman actually had the nerve to ask Elizabeth to the dance. I mean, we haven't even been broken up for a week! Did he really think she'd say yes?*

Then again, *he* was already asking other girls out. What if Elizabeth *did* say yes to Bruce?

Todd would go to bed and stay there for a month, that's what. With the covers pulled over his head.

"Be forever hero mine?" Mandy Miller stared at Elizabeth with a skeptical expression on her face. The *Sixers'* lovegram table was set up in a corner of the cafeteria. It was Thursday, the last day to get in an order before the final Valentine's Day issue. "Look, Elizabeth—I like Peter Jeffries and all, but we're not even officially going out. I can't send him a lovegram that says, 'Be forever hero mine'!"

Elizabeth held up her hands and grinned. "I know. It's a little over the top," she admitted. "But Valentine's Day is your chance to say things you wouldn't normally say. That's what makes it such a great holiday. The hero line makes it sound like you're a medieval princess or something and Peter is your knight."

Mandy bit her lip. "But Peter isn't my knight," she protested. "He's just a nice guy in my English class."

"I know," Elizabeth said with a smile. "That's what he is now. But can you picture him transformed into a knight? Just for you?" She raised her eyebrows hopefully. "Maybe with a little work, we'll get him to think of cupids and roses."

"I don't want him to think of cupids and roses," Mandy protested. "I just want him to think I'm nice!"

"Nice?" Elizabeth repeated.

"Nice," Mandy said again. "What's wrong with that?"

"Nothing," Elizabeth assured her. "It's just that it's a little . . . lukewarm."

"Look, Elizabeth," Mandy said patiently. "I just want to send Peter a *nice* lovegram that will make him think I'm *nice* and that I kind of *like* him. That's all. Can you do it?"

"Of course we can do it, Mandy," Randy Mason,

who sat next to Elizabeth, said quickly, before Elizabeth could answer. "Look, you just write exactly what you want to say on this form, and we'll make sure it gets in tomorrow's issue. OK?"

"OK." Mandy plunked down her dollar fifty and began writing her lovegram.

After she left, Randy turned to Elizabeth. "Listen, Elizabeth, I know that you're really into this romance stuff, but I'm sensing that some people just aren't comfortable with all the mushiness."

"I don't think it's all that mushy," Elizabeth said, defending herself. "I just think people shouldn't be afraid to explore the real romance of Valentine's Day."

"That's just it, Elizabeth," Randy went on. "It seems like sometimes you want them to have feelings that you think they have, but they don't think they have them." He looked confused. "Or something. Anyway, this isn't really like you." He peered at her over his glasses. "Usually, you're so levelheaded."

Elizabeth sank down lower in her chair and sighed. "I'm sorry, Randy. I don't know what's wrong with me. For some reason I just got totally excited about Valentine's Day this year." She buried her head in her hands. "Maybe I'm just trying to have a love life by making other people have one. Maybe I'm just losing my mind," she said sadly.

Randy patted her on the back. "It's OK, Elizabeth," he said. "Don't worry about it. You're one of the nicest people I know, and everyone thinks Todd is being totally lame. Just, you know, cool it a bit on the romance stuff."

Elizabeth gave him a tiny smile. "OK, Randy. Thanks. I'll try."

"Elizabeth!" Aaron said with a smile, coming up to their table. "Just the girl I wanted to see. Have you had lunch yet?"

"No," Elizabeth said. "I was just about to go."

"We'll go together," Aaron said, motioning toward the line. "I need to talk to you."

"Hey," said Ken Matthews, coming up behind them. "Mind if I join you? I'll help you carry your tray, Elizabeth."

Elizabeth looked back at Randy, who winked at her.

"Well, OK," Elizabeth said as she, Aaron, and Ken moved into line.

"Check it out," Belinda Layton said, pointing to Elizabeth. Belinda and the other members of the Unicorn Club were eating lunch at their special table in the cafeteria, which they called the Unicorner. "Ever since Todd dumped her, every boy in school has been swarming around her. It's like ants on a candy bar or something."

"Tell me about it," Jessica said bitterly. "As if it

isn't bad enough that Aaron hasn't asked me to the dance. Now I have to sit here and watch him drool all over my sister in the lunch line. Do you know he actually *called* her the other night?"

"It *is* pretty weird," Mandy Miller admitted. "And Elizabeth's acting kind of bizarre, too. Just now I tried to send a lovegram to Peter Jeffries, and she was pushing me to get all mushy. I don't know what's going on. She's not really being herself."

"Has Peter asked you to the dance yet?" Jessica asked.

Mandy made a face. "Not yet."

Across the table, Janet winked at Jessica. "Who's on cheer duty today?" she asked. Lila, Jessica, Tamara, and Ellen raised their hands.

"And Winston and Amy Sutton," Ellen added, naming the two non-Unicorn Boosters.

"OK," Janet said, checking her watch. "Hurry up, guys. Ten minutes till today's cheers."

"And another thing," Jessica continued, "at least three guys have asked her to the dance, but she hasn't said yes to any of them. What's going on?" Jessica feared she already knew the answer—Elizabeth hadn't said yes to any of the invitations because she was already going with Aaron! What other explanation could there be? Aaron had called her the other night; Aaron hadn't asked Jessica yet; every time Jessica looked up, Aaron and Elizabeth were whispering about something. It was totally humiliating, not to mention heartbreaking.

Maybe you're jumping the gun, Jessica consoled herself as she took a bite of her turkey sandwich. She didn't want to get all worked up over nothing. After all, it was totally unlike Elizabeth to go behind her sister's back to date her sister's sort of boyfriend. On the other hand, Elizabeth did seem to have been bitten really hard by the romance bug this year. Maybe she was desperate to have a new Romeo, since her old Romeo had bailed out on her.

But she didn't have to take my Romeo, Jessica thought mournfully. *Just because we shared the Juliet role doesn't mean we have to share my boyfriend, too!*

Jessica sighed and put down her sandwich. The dance was only one day away, which meant that Aaron and Elizabeth had exactly one day to get their acts together before Jessica killed them both.

Jessica looked over at Lila, who seemed weirdly preoccupied by her chocolate milk. *She has to be the luckiest girl in the world,* Jessica thought enviously. Jessica would be so happy right now to have a fabulous, adorable, loyal, attentive, generous, and sweet boyfriend like Gray.

I wish all I had to worry about was my twin sister stealing my boyfriend, Lila thought bleakly as she sipped her chocolate milk. *In fact, if I did have a twin sister, I would gladly give her Gray, and good riddance.*

Lila stirred her chocolate milk around with her

straw as she thought about the miserable afternoon she'd spent yesterday after the Unicorns had left, convinced that Lila and Gray were a hot item once again. First she had yelled at Mr. Pratt's grandson. Then she had gone up to her room, but she hadn't had the energy to do anything but sit by her bedroom and watch that Jason-or-whatever-his-name-was person raking leaves in the yard from her bedroom window. Although he was a complete idiot, she had noticed that he was tall and seemed strong. For some reason, that made her even more irritated.

Lila rubbed her forehead. The dance was tomorrow. Tomorrow! What was she going to do?

Inside, she knew what she had to do. She couldn't go on like this. No, she simply had to come right out and tell the Unicorns the truth: there was no Gray, there never had been a Gray, there never would be a Gray. They would probably tease her, but in the end, they might be able to laugh about it. Of course, she'd be completely humiliated, but she'd just have to bear it till she was eighteen— then she could leave Sweet Valley and never show her face again. It was only six years away.

"Um, guys, you know about Gray?" Lila said in a small voice, looking down at her lunch tray.

"Oh, I wanted to ask you, Lila," Ellen began, opening a bag of carrot sticks. "I hate to keep bugging you about it, but—"

"Oh, right—Gray's friend," Lila said, suddenly remembering. She made an apologetic face. "I think you better plan on going with someone else," she said carefully. "Especially after what I'm about to tell you about Gray."

"We *know* all about Gray, Lila," Janet said impatiently. "But what I bet everyone *doesn't* know is that Sarah Thomas has been lying about her boyfriend, Seth."

"What?" Jessica leaned forward eagerly, ignoring Lila.

Tamara pushed her lunch aside and looked at Janet with wide eyes.

"Well," Janet said importantly, looking around at her audience, "you know how Sarah has been saying that Seth was fourteen and in ninth grade at Big Mesa High?"

Lila's ears pricked up. Sarah was only in sixth grade. Her "older man" had been big news.

"You mean Seth doesn't exist? She made him up?" Lila asked hopefully. Maybe she could turn this to her advantage.

"No, Seth definitely exists," Janet confirmed. "I've seen him with my own two eyes. And he's pretty cute, I have to admit. However, I happen to know for a fact that he's only twelve and in seventh grade at Big Mesa Middle School."

"You're kidding," Kimberly said with a gasp. "She's been lying about his age?"

"Yep," Janet said. "I guess he's not such an older man after all."

"I can't believe she would exaggerate like that," Jessica marveled. "It was so easy for her to be found out."

"Kind of pathetic," Tamara said coolly. "I'm glad the Unicorns are much too cool to do something that lame."

Ellen nodded. "Yeah. When you have to make up stuff just to look good in front of your friends . . ." She let her voice trail off meaningfully.

Janet looked at her friends steadily. "*Genuinely* cool people don't make up those sorts of lies."

"Yeah," Jessica agreed. "Genuine coolness takes more work, but it's worth it."

"Oh, wow, look at the time," Janet said, quickly pushing back her chair. "Everyone who's on cheering duty, let's go. Lila, what was that you were saying about Gray?"

"Oh, nothing," Lila said quickly, gathering all her trash into a ball. Her voice sounded high and breathy. "Nothing at all. That is, I don't remember. So anyway, what's our first cheer?"

Eleven

◇

OK, maybe she's shy, but this is ridiculous, Todd thought in frustration as he headed out the exit doors on Thursday afternoon. The dance was tomorrow, and his secret admirer still hadn't revealed herself. And even worse, he couldn't get the possibility of Elizabeth's dating Bruce Patman out of his mind. *It's not that she shouldn't be friends with another guy*, he reasoned. *But Bruce?* Todd was starting to feel sick.

On the walkway in front of school Todd spotted Elizabeth talking to Ken Matthews. Todd had noticed that a lot of his friends had been paying extra attention to her. *Well, fine. No problem*, he thought. He wouldn't want Elizabeth to feel lonely.

Elizabeth caught his eye. She blushed slightly and turned away.

Ken was telling some story and laughing. "And then the guy said, 'But that's *my* elephant!'"

Elizabeth chuckled, too. "That's really funny, Ken," she said. "We should put that in the *Sixers*."

It's nice of Ken to try to cheer her up, Todd thought. If Todd felt this bad, no doubt Elizabeth felt much worse.

Then, right over Elizabeth's shoulder, he spotted Sophia Rizzo. She was smiling right at him. He smiled back.

Sophia beckoned to Todd, and his heart lifted. *Is Sophia the one? Finally!*

Todd walked toward her, feeling pleased. He could definitely do a lot worse for himself than Sophia. She was really pretty and nice, even though she used to have kind of a tough reputation.

Todd felt a little flicker of annoyance at how long Sophia had kept him waiting, not revealing herself till the day before the dance, but he brushed that aside. The important thing was that she was crazy about him. It was obvious that he was her dream guy, and it wouldn't kill him to be nice to her.

"Oops, sorry," Patrick Morris said as he brushed past Todd and ran right toward Sophia.

Sophia smiled and took his hand. "Ready to go to Casey's?" she asked sweetly.

"Am I ever," Patrick said. "I've been waiting all day for this."

Sophia and Patrick walked off together, gazing into each other's eyes. Todd stood alone with his mouth hanging open.

"Have you girls decided what to wear to the dance tomorrow?" Mrs. Wakefield asked as the twins ate their after-school snack on Thursday.

"Oh, I don't know," Elizabeth said, biting into a cookie. "I still don't even know if I'm going or not. Maybe I'll just stay home and rent a movie."

"Jessica? What about you?"

Jessica shot a dark glance at Elizabeth. "I don't know if I'm going either. Obviously, Aaron is interested in *someone else*."

"What makes you think that?" Elizabeth asked, frowning in concern.

Jessica give her an exasperated look. "Oh, please. Do you think I'm *blind*? *Anyone* could see what's going on. I don't need to bang my head against the wall."

"What are you talking about?" Elizabeth pressed.

"Don't pretend you don't know!" Jessica snapped. "Everyone at school knows about it. And all I can say is, people who steal other people's boyfriends ought to be ashamed of themselves. Because the other people whose boyfriend she stole always know about it and they tell other people and then everyone realizes what kind of person the boyfriend stealer is and she ends up with no friends at all, even though she's the kind of person who people usually really like." She stopped, panting for breath,.

Elizabeth's eyes were wide with shock. "Jessica, I—"

"I don't want to hear anymore," Jessica snarled. She flung down her napkin and stomped out of the room.

"And if my slimy loser supposed boyfriend thinks he can get away with this, he's crazy," Jessica told Mandy on the phone. She had called Mandy as soon as she'd gotten to her room and flopped on her bed. "I'm going to call him tonight and let him know I'm onto him."

"Really?" Mandy asked. "You don't think it would be better to talk to him in person?"

Jessica rolled over on her back and switched ears. "Well, maybe," she said thoughtfully. "Maybe you're right. I want to *see* him squirm. And you know what?"

"Uh-uh. What?"

"I'm going to remind him of all the good times we've had together, all the fun things we've done," Jessica said with relish. "Then I'll say if he likes Elizabeth better than he likes me, he's welcome to her! You're right, Mandy. The dirty stinking rat deserves to be exposed in public—the more public the better. And so does my oh-so-innocent sister. Tomorrow at lunchtime, in the cafeteria."

"That's when you'll tell him all this?" Mandy asked, sounding awed. "Are you totally sure about Elizabeth? I mean, I know she's been being weird lately, but I sort of can't imagine her really doing this."

"Believe it," Jessica said confidently. "It's the only explanation. I'm going to tell them off right on Valentine's Day. Then everyone will know just how wronged I've been."

"Hmmm," Mandy said.

Jessica scooched around until she could put her socked feet up against the wall and hang her head over the side of her bed. This was a good position to think in.

"What do you think I should wear tomorrow?" she asked Mandy. "I want to make Aaron extra sorry."

"How about your denim mini?" Mandy suggested.

"Perfect," Jessica said.

Great. Four brilliant plans, and they all flopped, Lila thought despondently, as she wandered around the grounds of the Fowler estate on Thursday afternoon.

Miserably, she roamed through the small fruit orchard, and down the slope to the formal rose garden. There was a small bench there beneath a large arbor where Lila went to be alone. Now she slumped down on it dejectedly. Since it was only February, none of the roses were in bloom, but the bushes were covered with green leaves.

What am I going to do? she thought desperately. Tomorrow was the dance, and there was no way she could save herself from total and complete humiliation. If she said she and Gray had just broken up, the Unicorns would probably try to track him down to help them make up. If she told the truth, the Unicorns would brand her as so uncool she had to go around making up boyfriends.

She took a tissue out of her pocket and began to cry. She had to leave town. She had to join the witness relocation program. She would dye her hair, get colored contacts, and start over again, in some new town, some new state. Maybe Iowa. No one she knew would run into her there. She started crying even harder.

"Lila—Ms. Fowler. Are you OK?"

Horrified, Lila looked up through wet and spiky lashes to see the gardener's grandson, looking at her with concern. His green eyes peered into hers.

"I'm fine," Lila snapped shakily. "Go plant something." She turned her head a little so he couldn't see her cry. She should have known better than to come outside with Jason or Jeffrey or whatever his name was prowling around. What had she been thinking?

But instead of going away, he sat down right next to her on the bench. He was wearing baggy black jeans and a dark blue sweatshirt. His dark chestnut hair fell over his forehead.

"Tell me what's wrong," he said softly. "You sound so sad." Some pruning shears fell out of his pocket onto the ground, but he ignored them.

"None of your business," Lila said, wiping her eyes with her tissue. "There's nothing anyone can do to help, anyway."

"Come on, now," he said. "Tell ol' Justin all about it."

Justin. Right. "Why should I tell you?" Lila demanded.

"Well, for one thing," Justin said, "because there's no one else around. Besides, sometimes you can tell a stranger things that you wouldn't want your best friend to know."

At the idea of Jessica and all the other Unicorns' knowing about her pathetic failure of a love life, Lila burst into tears all over again. She was hardly conscious of Justin patting her shoulder comfortingly. Then, before she knew what she was doing, she found herself blurting out the whole, sordid story, right from the beginning. She told Justin all about her fantasy about arriving at the dance with Jake, and what they would both be wearing, and about how she had been so sure he would order a cheer for her.

"Then Jake said, Brooke Dennis," Lila sobbed, "and I was so embarrassed. Everyone was looking at me . . ."

"I understand," Justin said soothingly. He pulled a clean tissue out of his pocket and handed it to her. "Then what happened?"

"So I made up this Gray person," Lila sobbed. Gradually, she choked out all the horrible things she had gone through since Gray had appeared on the scene. "Now the dance is tomorrow, right in the Sweet Valley Middle School gym, at eight o'clock, and I have to show up alone!" Lila wailed. "My friends will be so mad at Gray for standing me up that they'll try to hunt him down. I bet they'll try to go to his house or hang out around Lovett Academy or something. They'll put an ad in the newspaper, trying to find him. That will be the worst of all!" Fresh tears coursed down her face.

"This wouldn't have happened if everyone had just minded their own business," Justin said, frowning in concern.

Lila's eyes widened. He really did understand. "Exactly! It wasn't really my fault. But everyone kept asking me questions."

"They practically forced you into it," Justin agreed firmly. He looked off into the rose garden, his forehead creased, as though he was thinking hard about something. Then his face cleared. "Hey, I have an idea," he said. "I don't know if you'll go for it, but—"

"Justin!" Mrs. Pervis's voice carried through the rose garden. "Justin Pratt, where are you?"

"You better go," Lila said, wiping her eyes one last time. "Thanks for listening. I didn't mean to bend your ear off."

"No problem," Justin said. "Try not to worry. I bet everything will work out."

"There you are!" Mrs. Pervis, red-faced and puffing after the long walk from the house, stood in front of them with her hands on her hips. "Justin, what in the world did you do to my pea plants? Come over here." She stomped off toward the kitchen garden.

With an apologetic look, Justin straggled after her, taking big strides to catch up.

Well, he may not be much of a gardener, Lila thought, watching Justin leave, *but he's a pretty nice guy.* Not that he'd really fixed anything. He'd told her not to worry, but of course she had to anyway. He'd listened to her problems, but she still had no way to get rid of her nonexistent boyfriend. Which meant that tomorrow night she was probably going to be laughed right out of the Unicorns.

Twelve

"Ah, Elizabeth, there you are," Mr. Bowman said, approaching her at her locker on Friday morning before homeroom. "Could I see you for just a moment in my office?"

"Sure," Elizabeth said, puzzled.

Once inside Mr. Bowman's office, Elizabeth sat down in one of the chairs facing Mr. Bowman's desk. He leaned against the edge of his desk.

"Elizabeth, I just wanted to talk to you about a few things," he said. "Today's issue of the *Sixers* came out, and, well, a student has mentioned to me that she's not very comfortable with how her lovegram reads."

Elizabeth felt her ears growing warm. "What do you mean?" she asked in a small voice.

"Well, this person feels that she sort of let herself

be swayed—or persuaded, rather—into sending a lovegram that was much more romantic than she intended." Mr. Bowman paused. "Now she regrets it, but it's too late, because the paper just came out."

For a moment Elizabeth sat frozen in her chair, embarrassed beyond belief. "I don't know what to say," she murmured finally, looking at the floor.

"Were you encouraging people to send very romantic lovegrams?"

"Well"—Elizabeth swallowed—"maybe just a tiny bit, once or twice. I mean, these are *lovegrams*. It's Valentine's Day. I just kind of wanted everyone to get into the spirit of the holiday. I didn't think anyone minded. Well, sometimes they minded just a little bit. But I never *forced* anyone into anything."

"I think maybe you got bowled over by the whole Valentine's spirit," Mr. Bowman said gently. "I know that many students liked and appreciated the help you gave them with their lovegrams, but if you tried to urge even one person a tiny bit too hard, then you weren't being very fair."

Elizabeth flushed and looked down at her feet. When he put it that way, she could see the problem. She guessed she would be pretty mad if someone had decided they knew her feelings better than she did. How had she made such a mistake?

Groaning softly, she put her head down on her

arms. This was the absolute worst Valentine's Day she'd ever had. For one thing, her boyfriend had dumped her. For another, Mr. Bowman was disappointed in her. And she could just imagine all the embarrassed middle-schoolers whose lovegrams were too romantic for them. Maybe she should just go home and crawl into bed.

"Now, Elizabeth," Mr. Bowman said, patting her shoulder, "this isn't a really big problem. I know you're usually much more sensitive to other people's feelings. I just wanted to point out the miscommunication, that's all. Don't worry about it. You better run along to class now. I'll see you in English."

"Yes, sir," Elizabeth said miserably, gathering up her backpack. She shuffled out of the office and down the hall to her homeroom. It was only eight thirty in the morning, and she already felt as if this were the longest day in her life.

In math class, Lila listlessly took out her textbook and a clean sheet of paper. Automatically she began to work the problems the substitute teacher had assigned.

"What's wrong with Mrs. Wyler?" Lloyd Benson asked, raising his hand.

The substitute smiled at him. "I'm afraid Mrs. Wyler had a mild appendicitis attack. She should be OK very soon. Now, if any of you have questions about the work assignment, just let me know." She sat down at Mrs. Wyler's desk and opened her textbook.

Lila began to write her figures in neat little columns. Math was one of her best subjects—her father said it ran in the Fowler family.

Mrs. Wyler is so lucky, she thought. *I wish I could have an appendicitis attack.* She started writing her answers at the bottom of the page. Then she snapped up her head.

Of course! Why hadn't she thought of that before? She *could* have an appendicitis attack. Nothing was stopping her—who would know? Yes, appendicitis was the perfect answer to all her problems.

Humming a little under her breath, Lila turned back to her decimals.

"They're both acting so innocent," Jessica grumbled that day at lunch as she and the other Boosters were changing into their uniforms. "That's what's really getting me. I've been dropping all kinds of hints, and showing them both how mad I am, but my double-crossing sister and my snaky boyfriend are acting like they don't even notice."

"Maybe you're jumping the gun a little bit, Jessica," Amy suggested, as she pulled on her Booster skirt. "I mean, for a couple of days I thought Elizabeth might be going after Ken. But it turns out it was completely innocent. Ken says he was only trying to cheer her up. And he and I *are* going to the dance together tonight. So maybe it's not Elizabeth's fault that all those guys have been flocking around her."

"Yeah, Jessica," Janet Howell said, pulling her hair back into a ponytail. "Maybe Aaron has been loyal to you all along. Maybe you don't know the whole story."

"Are you crazy?" Jessica squealed as she tied her sneakers. "Do I have to beat you on the head with it? My boyfriend and my sister are going to show up at the dance together tonight, and my life will be in shreds!"

Jessica saw Tamara and Janet exchange a glance. *They're acting like they know more about this than I do,* Jessica thought irritably. *Well, fine. I don't need their support.*

Snatching up her red-and-white pom-poms, she stormed out to the cafeteria. Maybe her friends weren't taking this seriously, but she was. Her own sister had betrayed her. Aaron was a total dunderhead. And she, Jessica Wakefield, didn't intend to take this lying down. Right after today's cheers, she was going to march over to Aaron's table and tell him just what she thought of him. Then she was going to take that piece of spice cake off Aaron's tray and throw it right into Elizabeth's face! That would show them.

*   *   *

"At least this Valentine's Day has been good for *some* of us," Jessica said to Lila a few moments later. They were standing in the cafeteria, waiting for the other Boosters to catch up, and Lila was swinging her pom-poms around, practicing a few moves. "I guess Gray is still being his wonderful self, huh?"

Lila grinned. "Yeah. I'm so lucky. He's just the most romantic guy I've ever met. I can't wait for everyone to meet him tonight at the dance," she said cheerfully.

Jessica scowled. "Well, don't count on me to be there," she said darkly. "I'll probably be home, trying to convince Mom and Dad to give Elizabeth up for adoption."

"Good luck," Lila said with a laugh.

As Janet and the other Boosters came out and got into formation in the front of the cafeteria, Jessica pasted a big Booster smile on her face and threw her head back. Her life was in shreds, but she wasn't about to be unprofessional.

Janet looked around, blew on her whistle, then let it drop down on its cord. "Ready, Boosters? First cheer!"

The Boosters all moved in a series of cancan kicks, then swung forward and back in a choreographed pattern. Janet and Kimberly stepped forward and led them in today's first cheer.

"Valentine's is here again.
My love is here to stay.
Maria Slater's my best friend
Forever and a day! Yay!"

Maria turned around in her seat, blushing and smiling. She leaned over to Tim Davis and whispered something to him, and he nodded and smiled at her.

The Boosters did some high kicks, and Amy and Jessica formed a mini-pyramid with Tamara.

As they regrouped and got ready for their second cheer, Jessica shot a look into the audience. *That's a switch. Aaron and Elizabeth aren't together,* she noticed. In fact, Elizabeth was sitting at a table by herself, looking pretty sad. *Well, good. She deserves a little misery after what she's done to me.*

Aaron was surrounded by a bunch of his friends, and they were laughing and joking around.

You won't be laughing much longer, you two-timer, Jessica thought angrily.

Janet blew her whistle again, and they started their second cheer.

"Bruce! Bruce! You're my ideal
No other boy compares!
If you believe my love is real
Meet me behind the stairs!"

The Boosters all jumped high and did a little shimmy, then Janet unrolled a scroll. "From . . . Anonymous! See you at three thirty," she read in a mysterious voice.

The cafeteria erupted in hoots and yells. Bruce looked around, an arrogant smile on his face.

"Who sent that?" Jessica whispered, moving closer to Janet.

"*Well*," Janet whispered back, smiling slyly, "none other than Caroline Pearce. Probably not exactly the secret admirer of Bruce's dreams, huh?"

As the Boosters prepared to wind things up for the day, Lila moved off to the side of the cafeteria and pressed her hand to her forehead, hoping she looked pale. It was time to have appendicitis.

"Ohhh," she moaned softly. She looked around. No one seemed to have heard her—they were all listening to Janet read off how much money the Boosters had made doing their cheers-for-hire.

"We have enough to hire the photographer for tonight's dance!" Janet announced proudly, and the cafeteria erupted in applause.

"Ohhh!" Lila moaned a little louder, pressing her hand against her side, and wobbling toward the middle of the cafeteria, where someone would be sure to notice her.

"Our money, along with the money from the

Sixers' lovegrams, means tonight's dance will be the best the middle school has ever seen!" Janet yelled.

Students cheered and waved their arms.

This is it. Time for me to drop. Lila was a little scared about what she was going to do, but clearly she had no choice. She took a few more steps into the middle of the cafeteria, forming her face into a grimace. Taking a deep breath, she tried to make her knees wobble. *OK, Lila. One, two, three, down.*

Thirteen

◇

As Lila prepared to drop to the floor in a fit of appendicitis, Jessica left the Boosters and stalked across the cafeteria toward Aaron.

"Aaron Dallas, I have something to say to you!" she yelled, her voice echoing all over the cafeteria as she stood in front of him with her hands on her hips.

Lila craned her neck to see what was going on. *I'll fall down in a second. What is Jessica doing?*

"Quick, everybody!" Janet Howell hissed, and the Boosters immediately jumped into position.

What's going on? Lila wondered. *I thought the cheers were over.* She stumbled out of the way, trying to keep a grimace on her face.

The Boosters all moved in a grapevine to the left, and then to the right. Lila stood on the side and watched. No one was paying attention to her at all. Jessica had stopped what she was about to say and was staring at the Boosters.

I could be dying, Lila thought sadly. *I could be dying of appendicitis, and no one would care or even notice.*

What are they doing? Jessica wondered. *We're supposed to be done for today.*

She watched in confusion as the Boosters launched into a cheer:

> "Oh, Jessica, oh, Jessica,
> You make my heart beat fast.
> You've always been the twin for me,
> From first until the last."

Jessica stared at the Boosters. A deep blush spread up her neck to her face as the Boosters wove in and out of a small square, chanting this huge, custom-made cheer.

> "I love the way you chew your gum,
> Right in our science class.
> Around you I am never glum,
> Not even when you sass.
> Your long blond hair is like the sun,
> Your eyes are like the sky.
> With you I have terrific fun,

I'd never make you cry.
You take a joke just like a boy,
You look just like a girl.
I'd follow you to Illinois,
Or all around the world.

The Boosters put their arms around each other in a line and did alternating kicks, then split up and formed a five-person pyramid.

"I can't compete with Johnny Buck;
He sure gives me a blister.
And now I find, with just my luck,
You think I like your sister.
But Jessica, you must believe,
There is no other one.
I'd like to take you out tonight
In order to have fun.
Please say you'll be my date tonight,
I'll bring you one red rose.
There's no way I'll be late tonight,
Or step upon your toes."

The Boosters all swarmed into a little circle and yelled, "Be my Valentine, Jessica! Love, Aaron! Yay!" Then they all jumped up and down, doing splits, and the whole cafeteria erupted into cheers and clapping.

Jessica stood in front of Aaron, her eyes misty

with tears. It was by far the longest, most special cheer the Boosters had done in the last week. And it had all been for her.

"What were you going to say, Jessica?" Aaron asked.

"Nothing," she said, her voice cracking. "Only that I'll be happy to go to the dance with you tonight." At that everyone cheered and clapped some more.

"I feel faint," Lila said, trying to make her voice shake. She was standing off to one side, and she moved closer to the Boosters. "I think I have a fever."

"We are so awesome!" Kimberly shouted as she and Janet high-fived.

"You said it!" Tamara agreed.

"Let's hear it for Aaron and Jessica!" Mandy exclaimed, and the cafeteria was filled with another burst of shouting and applause.

"Ohhh," Lila moaned, clutching her side. She reached out with her hand as though trying to steady herself. "Ohh . . . everything is going black. What's happening to me?" Her eyelids fluttered, as if she were about to pass out.

She looked around. A huge crowd was swarming around Jessica and Aaron. *I'm about to die of appendicitis, and they're the biggest news of the day?* she thought incredulously. Apparently, she could just drop dead right there and no one would care.

She stood up, put her hands on her hips, and glared at her so-called friends. *So much for that plan,* she thought gloomily.

This was it. She had no excuse not to be at the dance tonight. She was supposed to bring a guy who didn't exist. And her career as a Unicorn was about to be over.

"Will you ever forgive me, Lizzie?" Jessica asked that night as she was laying out her clothes for the dance.

Elizabeth smiled sadly at Jessica. "Of course. I guess there was no way for you to know I was just giving Aaron information that he could put in your cheer." She paused. "Even though you should have trusted me. Even though you should have known I'd never do that to you."

Jessica made a rueful face. "I know. It was stupid of me. But in a way, it's all Aaron's fault. If he had just asked me to the dance days ago, like he should have, none of this would have happened."

Elizabeth slumped down on Jessica's bed, watching as Jessica tried on different accessories. All afternoon Elizabeth had been trying to decide whether to go to the dance or not. Now that she and Jessica had made up, she would have at least one person to talk to.

But she decided it would be smarter to stay

home. Why subject herself to more heartache? After all, Todd would be at the dance tonight. She wondered who he'd finally asked.

Elizabeth sighed. She knew she could have gone to the dance with some other boy—she'd had at least two acceptable invitations—but she really just wanted to go with Todd. Even if he was being an incredible jerk.

"Elizabeth, aren't you going to get ready? We have to leave in an hour." Jessica looked at her in the mirror.

"I'm not going," Elizabeth said firmly.

"What do you mean?" Jessica came and sat beside her on the bed. "You have to come tonight. It won't be any fun without you."

Elizabeth shook her head. "You have Aaron, and the rest of your friends. But I don't really feel like seeing Todd dancing with every girl at Sweet Valley Middle School."

"Elizabeth Wakefield, I'm surprised at you," Jessica said sternly. "I can't believe you're letting some stupid, boring boy get you down. It was partly your hard work that made the dance possible in the first place. Don't you want to see what you accomplished? And since when do you need Todd to have fun?"

"Well, since never, I guess," Elizabeth admitted softly.

"Look," Jessica continued. "Aaron and I will hang

out with you, and we'll all dance together. OK?"

Elizabeth gave her a small smile. "Well . . ."

"Come on," Jessica wheedled. "Please? Pretty please with sugar on top?"

Elizabeth couldn't help laughing. No one could beg like Jessica when she set her mind to it. And maybe her sister was right—she could have fun anyway. She didn't need Todd. As long as she had Jessica by her side, she could handle anything.

"OK," she relented, standing up. "You win. I'll go tonight."

"Yay!" Jessica cheered, giving her a hug. "Now, go get changed. And hurry up. I don't want to keep Aaron waiting. And I *definitely* don't want to miss Lila and Gray's dramatic entrance. Wait till you see her outfit—it's incredible."

Smiling, Elizabeth went through the bathroom into her room to get ready.

Todd lay flopped on his bed, banging his feet gently against the wall. He knew that the dance would be starting soon, but he wasn't really paying attention to the time. Somone tapped at his door.

"Come in," he called.

His mother opened the door. "Todd, why aren't you getting ready? Aren't you going to the dance tonight?"

Todd frowned darkly into his pillow. "I don't know."

His mother looked at her watch. "Well, it's almost seven now. You'd better make up your mind. Your dad or I will give you a ride."

"Yeah, OK," Todd said, not raising his head.

Looking concerned, his mother left the room and closed the door quietly.

Todd flipped over on his back and stared at the ceiling. His secret admirer had never revealed herself. He wondered if the whole thing had been a joke. But that poem had sounded so sincere. Sliding off his bed, he went to his desk and pulled it out again.

Dear Todd,
I've often wished that I could show
How you pierced my heart with Cupid's bow,
But we've been friends for far too long
For you to buy my siren's song.

Oh, Todd, so deep your eyes of brown.
I pray I see our friendship's grown.
I pray I see your understanding
For the love my heart's commanding.

On this, the feast of Valentine,
Please say your heart feels just like mine.
With wings of air I look ahead

Toward a day with joys unsaid,

And then I'll know we two won't part
Because I've given you my heart.

With love from . . .

Todd shook his head. There was no way this
could be a joke. This poem was definitely written
by someone who totally had the hots for him. But
who? All week he had tried to make himself available and approachable, in case his secret admirer
needed encouragement.. But all he'd done was
make a fool of himself.

Wait a minute, Todd thought suddenly. What if
his note writer was at the dance tonight. What if
she was waiting for him? What if she felt she
needed the security of a whole crowd before she
could reveal her identity? After all, it would be
much easier to come up to him when there was a
whole bunch of people around, dancing and having fun. *Yes!* Todd thought excitedly. Tonight could
be the night—a new beginning of a whole new
friendship.

Suddenly Todd saw himself in the mirror over
his desk. Who was he kidding? Hadn't he gotten
his hopes up over and over again only to make an
idiot out of himself? He didn't know who the note
was from, but it was obviously someone who had

no intention of ever telling him who she was. She probably just had a one-time burst of passion or something. It wasn't like she actually wanted to go out with him.

And besides, a voice at the back of mind said, *could any girl really hold a candle to Elizabeth?*

Todd buried his face in his hands. What an idiot he was. Elizabeth was one of his best friends, one of the nicest and prettiest girls he knew, and he had thrown her away like used Kleenex.

Crumpling up the note, he threw it angrily into the wastepaper basket. That note had ruined his life. He wished he'd never gotten it at all.

Probably there was no getting Elizabeth back. Ever since he had broken up with her, guys had been swarming all over her, begging her to go out with them. Guys like stupid Bruce Patman.

Todd groaned miserably. He knew there was only one thing to do: he had to go to the dance to ask Elizabeth's forgiveness. It might be totally humiliating, but he would apologize to her in front of everyone. Maybe she would take pity on him and even spare him one dance, if she thought it wouldn't hurt her new boyfriend's feelings.

Fourteen

I'll be sick, Lila decided at seven o'clock on Friday. *Yes, that's it. A cold. No, the flu. Yeah. I've been feeling incredibly queasy since I got home from school this afternoon, and there's no way I can go to any dance.* She took off her shoes and got into bed, pulling the covers up to her chin. She knew this plan wasn't really original, but it was all she could come up with at this point.

She sighed, thinking sadly of her adorable outfit hanging in the closet and of all the excitement at school over Valentine's Day. And here she was, pretending to be sick on the night of the hottest dance of the year. She, Lila Fowler. It was pathetic.

Since her father was away on his business trip, Mrs. Pervis was still in the house. Lila figured it would be best if Mrs. Pervis came looking for her and found her in bed. She should definitely be too sick to go downstairs and find the housekeeper herself. Maybe Mrs. Pervis would fix her a nice little tray and let her eat in bed.

Lila practiced a few small whimpers and moans. The thermometer was already by her bed, just in case.

Just as Lila expected, Mrs. Pervis soon knocked on her door.

"Come in," Lila croaked weakly.

"Lila! Why are you in bed?" the housekeeper exclaimed in her forthright way. "Don't you have a big school dance tonight?"

Lila nodded morosely, putting her hand to her forehead. "Yes, but I'm afraid I'm too sick to go," she mumbled. "I feel terrible."

"But your father—" Mrs. Pervis broke off. "Your father just got home from his trip. I'll send him in to see you. In the meantime, let's see if you have a fever."

Expertly, the older woman shook down the thermometer and pushed it into Lila's mouth. "I'll be back to check it in a minute. Let me tell your father you're ill."

Lila nodded a tiny bit, as though even the motion of moving her head were too painful to bear. As soon as Mrs. Pervis was gone, Lila turned on her bedside lamp and gently touched the thermometer to the lightbulb for just a second. She put it in her mouth just as Mrs. Pervis bustled back into the room.

"Let's see now," the housekeeper said, squinting to read the glass tube. "Ah, uh-huh . . . just as I suspected."

"What?" Lila moaned softly.

"You have a fever of one hundred and nine degrees," Mrs. Pervis said shortly, peering at Lila over the top of her glasses. "I'm surprised your brain hasn't exploded by now. Looks like a case of the plague to me. I think we better get you to the hospital right away and start you on intravenous fluids."

Lila stared at her in horror. She hated hospitals, and she hated needles.

Mrs. Pervis smiled. "Let me tell your father that you're on death's door. I'm sure he'd want to know." Turning, she left the room again.

Lila huddled down under her covers. Somehow she got the feeling that Mrs. Pervis wasn't exactly taking her seriously. How could that thermometer-to-the-lightbulb trick have failed her?

Just then her father appeared in the doorway, posing dramatically. He was wearing a beautiful, fancy black tuxedo with tails. Around his waist was a pink cummerbund covered with tiny white hearts. His pink bow tie matched.

"Look," he said, pulling at his neck. "It's a real tie, not a clip-on. I tied it myself. Impressed?" He looked around playfully, then noticed her tucked into bed. "Lila, honey, what are you doing? We have to be at the dance in twenty minutes!" he said, coming to sit beside her.

"We?" Lila said faintly.

"Yep!" her father said excitedly. "Remember when I called you at school to tell you about my business trip? I mentioned that I would be back Friday with a surprise."

Lila nodded suspiciously.

"The surprise is that I'm going to be one of the parent chaperons at the dance," he said proudly. "And Fowler Enterprises is providing all the fancy catered food."

"What?" Lila whispered in shock. She hadn't thought her nightmare could get any worse, but it had. Now her father had to be at the dance to witness her humiliation?

"Yep. We're having little crab puffs, and little sausages, and fruit and cheese and seven kinds of cookies. I thought you'd be so excited. I did it just for you—so we'd have some time together."

"I, uh . . ." Lila couldn't disappoint her father. He'd obviously gone to so much trouble. *So this is what it feels like. The end of my life.*

"Come on, now," her father said briskly. He held his hand out to her to help her out of bed. "Put on that revoltingly expensive outfit you bought that you'll probably wear only once, and let's go. I'll tell Richard to fire up the limo." Mr. Fowler strode out of her bedroom, looking tall and handsome.

Lila buried her head in her hands for a minute. Then she stood up, took off her school clothes, and pulled out her new outfit. She slipped into the sleek velvet bodysuit, the bell-bottom pants, the new shoes. She added a sophisticated double string of pearls.

Standing in front of her bedroom mirror, Lila couldn't help giving herself an admiring smile. She looked great. It was a fabulous outfit, totally up-to-the-minute. And if she had to be brought to her execution tonight, she was glad that at least she would go stylishly.

She smiled with satisfaction at her reflection. She was a Fowler, and Fowlers never admitted defeat. If she played her cards right, she might find a few aces up her sleeve. Now for the hair.

"Everything looks amazing!" Jessica exclaimed as soon as she, Elizabeth, and Aaron arrived at the Sweet Valley Middle School gym.

Elizabeth had to agree with her. Walled Temple, the local band the music committee had hired, was up on the stage. The decorations committee had gone all out, and everywhere were red, pink, and white balloons, red, pink, and white streamers, and red, pink, and white confetti. The refreshment tables had tablecloths that were covered with hearts, and large cardboard cutouts of cupids, hearts, and kissy-lips were taped all over the walls.

"Look, there's the photographer," Elizabeth said,

pointing to where a professional-looking woman was setting up a small cast-iron bench in front of a large poster covered with hearts.

Aaron bowed in front of Jessica. "May I have this dance, fair Jessicia?"

Jessica smiled and glanced at Elizabeth with her brows raised.

"Go, go," Elizabeth said, pushing them toward the dance floor. She was glad of their support, but she didn't want them to baby-sit her all night.

Feeling someone tapping her shoulder, Elizabeth turned around to see Amy.

"You look great, Elizabeth," Amy said. "I'm really glad you decided to come tonight."

Elizabeth smiled. She hadn't spent time with Amy this week. And she'd been so caught up in that Valentine's spirit that she'd almost forgotten that friends were what really mattered. "Thanks, Amy," she said warmly. "I'm glad I'm here, too."

"There's Ellen," Jessica said to Aaron after they'd had one dance. "Let me go talk to her, OK?"

"I'll go find Ken or Todd," he said.

Jessica ran over to where Ellen was taking a cookie from the refreshment table. Kimberly, Tamara, and Mandy were there, too.

"Have you guys seen Lila yet?" Jessica asked excitedly. "I can't wait to see Gray."

"Me neither," Ellen said, taking a bite of her

cookie. "I've heard so much about him, I feel like I know him already."

"I wonder if he's as cute as Lila said," Kimberly mused.

Jessica nodded emphatically. "He's probably even better," she said excitedly. "They're going to be so adorable together. I can't wait to see them slow-dance. It'll be so romantic."

Now that Aaron had come through for her, she wasn't at all jealous of Lila and Gray. Gray sounded fabulous, of course, but she didn't think anyone could actually be more romantic than Aaron.

"This is probably the most exciting dance the middle school has had yet," Tamara declared, helping herself to some punch. "Look at the guitar player—he's so cute!"

"He must be at least seventeen," Jessica scoffed. "Totally ancient!"

"Hey, there's Lila!" Ellen squealed, pointing toward the door.

"She looks gorgeous!" Mandy exclaimed.

"Gray must be drooling," Kimberly added.

"So where *is* Gray?" Jessica asked.

Standing near the doorway of the gym, Lila took a deep breath and nervously ran her hands down the sides of her black bell-bottom hiphuggers. She waited for her father, who was a few paces behind her, giving the chauffeur instructions on when to pick them up.

As her father reached her side, she took his arm, tossed back her hair, and walked sedately into the dance. The crowd seemed to part for her, and she could feel hundreds of pairs of eyes on her. Casually, she smiled up at her father, and he patted her hand. She knew she probably looked cool, calm, and collected—just the way she wanted.

Her father left her to go start his chaperon duties as some of the Unicorns ran up to her.

"Lila, you look fabulous!" Jessica said. "I knew that outfit was you."

Lila smiled graciously. "Thanks. I'm glad you pointed it out to me." She looked around. "The decorations committee did a terrific job. How's the band?"

"Great!" Tamara exclaimed. "The guitar player is a total babe."

Lila took another deep breath. She noticed that they were all looking at her expectantly. She knew the question that was coming—it was only a matter of seconds.

"So where's Gray?" Jessica blurted.

Lila smiled and shrugged a little. "Oh, Gray is running a tiny bit late," she lied. "He and his parents were down in San Diego today, but he promised me he wouldn't miss the dance. I talked to him a few hours ago, and he was at the airport, chartering a plane just for himself."

Mary Wallace and Mandy Miller let out dreamy sighs.

"So romantic," Jessica said, looking impressed.

"So devoted," Janet simpered.

"So expensive," Tamara moaned.

"Yes, well." Lila shrugged again. "I hope he gets here soon. He's so excited about meeting all my friends."

They're really cute, Elizabeth thought happily as she watched Jessica and Aaron pose for the Valentine's photographer a short while later. Jessica was beaming into the camera. Aaron tickled her, and she laughed. Flash!

Still laughing, they got up, and Bruce Patman sat down by himself, since he had come to the dance stag. Flash!

"So what lucky girl wants this picture?" Bruce said, sneering into the crowd.

"Your mother, probably!" Ken Matthews suggested.

Elizabeth laughed. This dance was turning out to be kind of fun.

Other couples were lined up to have their pictures taken: Amy and Ken, Maria Slater and Tim Davis, Grace Oliver and Winston Egbert.

When Grace and Winston sat down, Winston made bunny ears behind Grace's head.

"Cut it out, Winston!" Grace said, laughing. People in the crowd whooped and cheered. Flash!

"Elizabeth?" someone said over her shoulder.

Elizabeth turned to see Melissa McCormick standing in front of her. Elizabeth flushed, remembering that Melissa was the girl Elizabeth had convinced to send a romantic lovegram.

"Melissa," Elizabeth began, "I have to apologize to you. I never meant to ignore your feelings or embarrass you. I just thought—I don't know. I got carried away, I guess. I'm sorry. I hope Tom McKay understood that you didn't mean it." She hung her head. "I guess I should really apologize to him, too."

Melissa took Elizabeth's hand. "No, no, Elizabeth—that's what I wanted to tell you. I'm the one who should apologize to you," she said earnestly. "This morning, when the *Sixers* came out and I saw my lovegram, I suddenly panicked, I admit. I told on you to Mr. Bowman," she admitted. "I'd decided I had no chance with Tom, and I was so mortified to see that romantic message to him."

Elizabeth looked down at her feet guiltily.

"But guess what?" Melissa continued excitedly. "When Tom saw it, he told me that he'd wanted to be friends with me for a while, but wasn't sure if I liked him. Now we're here at the dance together! And it's all thanks to you. So thank you, Elizabeth. Without you, Tom and I would both be here alone, feeling miserable."

"Really?" Elizabeth said, looking at Melissa. "You're not mad?"

"Definitely not!" Melissa said. "But I'm sorry I

complained to Mr. Bowman. I wish I hadn't."

"That's OK," Elizabeth assured her. "I deserved it. And he was pretty nice about it. Anyway, I'm glad it all worked out."

Smiling, Melissa left her to go back to Tom McKay, who was holding her glass of soda.

Well! Elizabeth said to herself, taking a deep breath. *This is actually turning out to be a great Valentine's Day.* She looked excitedly around the gym, and as if drawn by a magnet, her eyes fell on Todd. He was gazing at her longingly and holding a bouquet of wildflowers and a heart-shaped box of candy.

That's weird, she thought. *I wonder where his date is?*

Suddenly Todd started to head purposefully in her direction.

Elizabeth stood there, unmoving. She jumped when someone took her arm.

"May I have this dance, Elizabeth?" Ken Matthews asked.

Behind him, Amy winked at Elizabeth.

Elizabeth managed a smile. "Yeah, I'd really like that."

Then she and Ken were moving into the middle of the dance floor, leaving Todd standing alone by the sidelines.

Fifteen

◇

"Oh, my gosh, is that him?" Jessica asked excitedly, pointing to a cute stranger across the room.

"No, that's not Gray," Lila answered. "I think that guy came with a seventh-grade girl. Gray will be here any minute, though." Shielding her eyes, she scanned the room. Then she gave a big smile far off into the distance. "There he is now! Let me just go talk to him for a minute, then I'll bring him right over to meet you."

Without another word she plunged into the crowd. Jessica craned her neck, but she couldn't even see Lila, much less any adorable guy who might be Gray.

"I can't wait to meet him," Janet said.

"Their whole love story is so romantic," Tamara agreed.

"It's almost too much to believe," Jessica said, wiggling with anticipation. "I don't think I've ever seen Lila so happy."

Thanks a lot, Ken, old buddy, Todd thought angrily as he watched Ken and Elizabeth head out to the dance floor.

"What's the matter, Wilkins?" Bruce said, appearing at Todd's side. "Did Cinderella ignore her pumpkin?"

"She didn't accept *your* invitation, Patman," Todd snarled. Bruce made a face and moved into the crowd.

Todd could feel other people's eyes on him. Everyone knew about his dumping Elizabeth, and now she was dancing with his best friend. They were all waiting for fireworks.

Then he looked at Elizabeth, dancing a fast dance with Ken. His eyes softened. She was wearing a deep-pink sweater and a matching long skirt. Her long blond hair fell softly around her shoulders, and her cheeks looked flushed. *She's never looked prettier,* he thought, with an unexpected lump in his throat.

Suddenly, he knew more than ever that if the prettiest, most popular girl in the whole school came up to him right then and said she was his secret admirer and was crazy about him, he just wouldn't care. It was Elizabeth he liked—it had always been

Elizabeth. True, sometimes she overreacted a little to perfectly innocent jokes, and sometimes she made a big deal out of something he thought wasn't worth bothering about. But she was a loyal friend. She would never have done to him what he had done to her last Monday in the library.

But she was more than loyal—she was also fun, and funny, and really smart. And right now, he thought she was the prettiest girl he had ever seen.

He looked down at the bouquet of wildflowers and the box he had brought. He looked back up to see Elizabeth and Ken dancing. He looked around to see all his friends and classmates staring at him, waiting to see what he would do. And then he knew.

"So where is he?" Ellen squealed, running up behind Lila, who had just rejoined the Unicorns.

Lila turned around with a big smile. "He had to call his parents and tell them he got here OK," she said confidently. "I said I'd meet him at the refreshment table. I hope he hurries up. I want us to have our picture taken."

"Yeah, that's a great idea," Jessica said enthusiastically. "Aaron and I had ours taken. I hope it comes out OK."

"Well, Gray will be back in a minute, and then we'll do it," Lila said.

"Great. I'm going to go grab Aaron for a quick

dance. Yell when Gray comes back," Jessica said, darting off into the crowd.

One by one the rest of the Unicorns left for a dance or to get refreshments. Lila checked her watch. What with Gray "arriving late" and then "making phone calls" and "getting refreshments," she had killed almost an hour and a half. The dance was supposed to last only another half hour or so. With any luck at all, Lila and Gray could "sneak away" for some romantic privacy, and he'd never actually meet her friends at all. Which was lucky, since he didn't exist.

Todd walked right out into the middle of the dance floor, through the masses of whirling bodies, until he reached Elizabeth and Ken.

"No, no, it's a zebra with measles, get it?" Ken was saying.

Summoning up all his courage, Todd tapped Ken on the shoulder. With a surprised jolt, Elizabeth and Ken stopped dancing and turned toward Todd. Elizabeth was still smiling at Ken's punch line. *I wish that smile were directed at me*, Todd thought longingly.

"Elizabeth—I, well, here." Todd thrust the wildflowers at her. "These are for you." He pushed the box of candy at her also.

Elizabeth frowned in confusion for a moment, then looked at Ken. "Would you excuse me?" she asked. Ken nodded, and then, without another glance at Todd, Elizabeth headed briskly through the crowd of people toward the refreshment table. Holding the flowers and candy, Todd followed her.

She picked up a paper cup of fruit punch and sipped it, watching the dance floor. Walled Temple started playing a slow song, and someone had dimmed the lights slightly.

Todd felt as though his stomach were somewhere around the tops of his sneakers. He was thrilled that she had at least agreed to talk to him, but she seemed so cold and far away.

He took a deep breath. "So who did you end up coming to the dance with?" he asked nervously.

"Jessica and Aaron," Elizabeth said, pointedly looking in the other direction.

Todd felt a rush of elation. After seeing all the attention Elizabeth had gotten this past week, he had been expecting her to come with a date.

"Elizabeth, please take the flowers and the candy," Todd asked humbly.

She gave him a cool glance. "No, thank you. I'm not interested in stuff you bought for some other girl."

Todd let out his breath in a short burst. "No, I got these just for you. There is no other girl. I know you like wildflowers, and I—I bought two boxes of candy and picked out all the strawberry creams and replaced them with nut ones, because you hate strawberry creams." He forced a crooked grin. "Would I do that for anyone else?"

"I don't know, Todd," Elizabeth said, gazing at him seriously. "Would you?"

Todd looked at his feet. "No," he said in an almost whisper. "Elizabeth, I've realized in the past few days just how wrong I was. I've really missed you, and I don't want to go out with anyone else. Can you ever forgive me for being so stupid?"

How much longer should I make him suffer? Elizabeth wondered, looking at Todd. She was kind of enjoying the way he was groveling like this in front of everyone. At the same time, she actually felt a little sorry for him. He seemed really sincere in his apology, and the wildflowers and the candy with the strawberry creams taken out showed that he was trying to be thoughtful. She felt herself softening toward him.

Reaching out, she took the wildflowers and inhaled their delicate fragrance. "These are really beautiful." Then she set them carefully on a table and opened the box of candy. She offered one to Todd. He took it, gazing at her with a hopeful, pleading expression.

"Please forgive me," Todd asked again.

Elizabeth let out a little sigh. Seeing him like this was incredibly satisfying. "Well, I'll try. I guess," she relented.

Immediately, Todd's face broke out into a huge smile. "I'll try to make it easy for you to try," he promised, then he held out his arms. "May I have this dance?"

"OK," Elizabeth said, a tiny smile on her face. She put down the box of candy. Walled Temple was playing another slow song, and the crowd parted to make way for Todd and Elizabeth. Several people clapped.

"It's so romantic," Elizabeth heard someone whisper as they went past.

"Of course it is," her friend whispered back. "That's the lovegram girl."

Feeling as though she were floating on happiness, Elizabeth drifted into Todd's arms, and they started to dance.

"I haven't even seen Gray yet," Jessica complained half an hour later. She and several other Unicorns were standing in front of the mirrors in the girls' bathroom. Jessica took out her brush and leaned over to fluff up her hair.

"I haven't either," Ellen said. "For a long time he was tied up with a guy he knew from Lovett Academy."

"He's not paying much attention to Lila," Janet observed with a frown. "Every time I see her, she's alone."

"Except they did take that long romantic walk

around the football field," Kimberly reminded her.

Jessica swung her hair up and watched it settle in a golden cloud around her shoulders. She was burning with impatience to meet Gray.

"You know what?" she said. "I have a great idea. Lila and Gray have had a hard week—what with breaking up and then making up and all. I think it would be nice to do something special for them. I mean, they *are* the most romantic couple at Sweet Valley Middle School." She blushed. "I mean, not counting me and Aaron, that is."

"After that humongous cheer, you better think so!" Ellen said. "It took me a whole day to learn that one."

Mandy and Jessica laughed.

"Yeah, but you know what I mean. Lila and Gray really fell for each other at first sight, and since then, it's been one thing after another with them," Jessica explained. "First Gray sent her those gorgeous flowers, and he calls her all the time, and then he paged her at school to make up, and then tonight he flew in all the way from San Diego just so he could spend Valentine's with her. So here's my idea." Jessica beckoned and the Unicorns moved in closer to her. "We'll go up to the lead singer of Walled Temple . . ." Jessica whispered.

"Brilliant," Ellen murmured a few minutes later.

"Fabulous," Janet concurred.

"Lila will be so thrilled," Kimberly said.

Jessica stood up, beaming with excitement. "I can't wait to see her face."

Todd and Elizabeth moved slowly around the dance floor, staring into each other's eyes. Elizabeth felt that her Valentine's dreams were finally coming true. She was here at the dance with the one boy she wanted to be with, and he was being satisfyingly humble. Everyone who had been mad about the lovegrams had forgiven her, and her girlfriends who thought she was after their boyfriends had realized she wasn't. Everything was falling into place.

"Are you having a good time?" Todd whispered in her ear.

"I am now," she answered, and he smiled. Then she put her head closer to his. "Oh, Todd, so deep your eyes of brown, I pray I see our friendship's grown," she whispered.

Todd gasped and stared at her. "You mean it was you? You all along?"

Elizabeth raised her eyebrows. "What do you mean?" she asked in surprise. "Of course it was me. Who would it be?"

Groaning, Todd dropped his head onto her shoulder. "Oh, gosh, am I stupid. Am I a moron."

She stared at him. "You mean you thought someone else . . ."

"Oh, Elizabeth, please forgive me. I'm so sorry.

I'm such an idiot. Why do you put up with me?" he moaned.

Elizabeth sighed and patted his shoulder. "'Cause you're such a snappy dresser," she said with a straight face.

"Thanks, Lila," Peter Jeffries said as they walked off the dance floor.

"Thank *you*, Peter," Lila said with a smile.

She checked her watch. *Yes!* Only about twenty-five more minutes to go. So far things had worked out pretty well. She was the only one who knew that Gray had never actually shown up.

Lila silently congratulated herself. Only a cool-headed, quick-thinking Fowler could have pulled off this miracle. And all she had to do was avoid her friends for a few more minutes. Then she could mumble some excuse about finding Gray, and the two lovebirds could disappear—for good.

"Like, I have an announcement to make," the lead singer for Walled Temple said into the mike as he flipped his hair out of his eyes.

The gym gradually fell silent as everyone turned and looked toward the stage. *What's this all about?* Lila wondered, sipping her glass of punch.

"I hope you little dudes and babes are having a good Valentine's Day," the singer continued.

Everyone cheered and clapped.

"We had a good time playing for you tonight. Be sure to look for our new CD, which should be out later this spring. It's called *Only in My Sneakers' Dreams*."

The gym erupted in more applause.

"Now, the students of Sweet Valley Middle School would like to congratulate the Valentine Couple of the Year," the singer announced dramatically. He looked down at the slip of paper in his hand.

Lila couldn't help laughing to herself. Whose harebrained idea had *this* been?

"In recognition of romance, devotion, and triumph over adversity," the lead singer read, "could the following people please come to the middle of the dance floor for a special last dance? Everyone give a big hand for . . . Lila Fowler and Gray Williams! Valentine Couple of the Year! All right!" The lead guitarist clapped his hands along with everyone else, his long hair falling back into his eyes.

Sixteen

◇

Lila felt her heart thud to a stop. A sickening knot formed in her stomach as a bright spotlight shone on her. On Lila Fowler, standing there alone. The clapping and cheering grew louder.

This can't be happening, Lila thought numbly, hardly able to see anything because of the spotlight in her eyes. *This simply can't be happening to me.* Everyone in the entire school was waiting eagerly for Gray to step to her side for the final dance by the Valentine Couple of the Year. Right now only Lila knew that he would never show, never take her hand, never whisper sweet nothings in her ear. Because he was a figment of her imagination.

Please let this be a nightmare. Please let me wake up and realize that I've only been dreaming. Then I'll never, ever lie again. I will have learned my lesson. I promise.

All her schoolmates, every one of her friends, every person from every class—they were all still clapping and cheering. But now, through the cheers, Lila could make out the slow rumble of people whispering, "Where is he?" Through the bright light she could barely make out the quick motions of heads turning to look for the mythical Gray.

And Lila stood there alone, in her fabulous, expensive outfit, in her adorable brand-new shoes, with her hair brushed and shiny. Alone.

"Look," Jessica whispered. "She's so excited she can't even move!"

Janet stood next to Jessica in the crowd, shaking her head and smiling. "She must be really thrilled. I bet she just can't believe it," she said, giggling.

I just can't believe this, Lila thought. Long minutes passed. Gray was still a no-show.

"OK, what's going on? What is she doing?" Jessica hissed to Janet. "Where's Gray?"

At least two minutes had gone by, and Gray was nowhere to be seen. The loudspeaker for the PA system crackled to life. "Gray Williams, please come to the dance floor. Gray Williams, please come to the dance floor."

"What's wrong with Gray?" Tamara demanded.

"Doesn't he know Lila's waiting for him?"

"I don't know," Jessica said. "But he's being really inconsiderate."

"He's been that way all night," Janet said with a frown. "I haven't seen them together once."

"Me neither," Belinda Layton agreed. "He's kind of being a jerk. An invisible jerk."

"An invisible jerk . . ." Jessica repeated under her breath as she stared out at Lila. Jessica and Lila had been best friends for years, and Jessica figured she knew Lila better than anybody. Right now Lila didn't look happy. She didn't look excited. She looked totally and completely mortified.

"Oh, no!" Jessica gasped. Suddenly the pieces of the mystery began to fall into place. No wonder she had never met Gray! No wonder he'd been off doing something else all night!

She met Janet's steady, serious gaze. "There is no Gray," Janet whispered, suddenly understanding also. "Lila's been lying this whole time!" An angry looked crossed her face. "She's been lying to all of us!"

"Poor Lila!" Jessica said in a low voice. "What made her do something so stupid?"

"Stupid is right," Janet said furiously. "Stupid and completely unacceptable for a Unicorn. We can't let her get away with this!"

Jessica shook her head emphatically. "Listen, Janet. We can't let a Unicorn be humiliated like this in front of the whole school. We can make Lila pay later, but right now we have to get her out of this mess!"

Janet frowned and looked around the gym. People had stopped clapping—the crowd was buzzing with confused whispers. "You're right, Jessica. The Unicorn image is on the line."

"Lila, why didn't you tell us?" Janet hissed. The Unicorns had gathered around Lila on the dance floor, shielding her from the crowd. "You're giving all the Unicorns a bad name."

"We'll deal with that later," Jessica insisted. "Right now let's get her out of here."

Looking around at her friends' faces, Lila felt her eyes well up with tears. She had been so stupid. Her pride had gotten her into this mess, and now there was no way out.

"I—I don't know what to say," Lila stammered as a tear rolled down her cheek. "I just—"

"Excuse me, excuse me!"

Lila broke off as someone started pushing his way through the huddle of Unicorns. Someone tall, with wavy, dark-chestnut hair and beautiful green eyes. He was wearing black jeans, a white tuxedo shirt open at the neck, and a tapestry vest. An untied bow tie dangled around his neck.

Lila stared. *He's adorable. He's incredible. He's . . .*

"Who are you?" Janet demanded.

The boy smiled, dazzling Lila with his even white teeth.

"I'm Gray," he said confidently. "Gray Williams, from Lovett Academy. Hasn't Lila mentioned me to you? You're the Unicorns, right?"

Janet, Jessica, and the rest of the Unicorns gazed at each other, their mouths hanging open in shock.

Gray faced Lila. "I'm really sorry, Lila," he said. "I didn't hear them calling me at first. Forgive me?" He turned back to the Unicorns. "If you'll excuse us, Lila and I have this dance."

The crowd around them erupted into cheers and applause once again, and Walled Temple began playing a slow, romantic song.

Then Gray gently took Lila in his arms. She rested her head on his shoulder, and they began to sway in time to the music.

"That has to be Gray," Janet said, her eyes practically popping out of her head as the Unicorns drifted to the edge of the crowd to watch. "He looks just like she described him."

"But where did he come from?" Jessica asked, looking at the couple in a daze. "Where has he been all night?"

Ellen shook her head, a look of amazement on her face. "It's like he appeared from nowhere—like in a fairy tale or something."

Mandy sighed dreamily. "They're absolutely

perfect together. Definitely the Valentine's Couple of the Year."

"I *knew* he had to be around here somewhere," Janet said with a satisfied smile. "A Unicorn wouldn't have gotten herself into such a stupid mess."

"This is the best Valentine's Day ever," Lila murmured, looking up into Justin Pratt's eyes.

He grinned. "So you don't mind dancing with a lowly gardener? You don't think I should be rooting around in the dirt or something?"

Lila blushed. "I don't know what you're talking about," she said primly, then smiled shyly. "There's no one I'd rather be dancing with."

Justin gazed at her. "And there's no one I'd rather be dancing with. It's worth messing around with all those pea plants."

Lila blushed again. "Thank you," she said softly as she put her head back on his shoulder. "I really learned my lesson, though," she said dreamily. "I sure won't make this mistake again."

"Maybe from now on you won't have to just *pretend* you have a boyfriend," Justin murmured.

Smiling happily, Lila looked up into his eyes.

"Hey, kids!"

Lila and Justin turned around just as the photographer was aiming her camera at them. As the flashbulb went off, Justin leaned over and kissed Lila's cheek.

I'm in heaven, Lila thought happily. *Sheer heaven.*

"So Lila and her date looked pretty happy at the final dance," Todd said after the dance, gently taking Elizabeth's hand. They were sitting on a bench outside of school, right in a puddle of cream-colored light, waiting for the Wilkinses to come take them home. Jessica and Aaron were going to go with the Wakefields.

"Yeah," Elizabeth agreed. It was chilly, and she edged closer to Todd. "Jessica said there's a romantic story behind it that she'll tell me later."

Todd grinned. "Valentine's sure has shaken things up around here. I'll be glad when things are back to normal."

"Me, too," Elizabeth said. "I'm ready to recover from my case of Valentine's fever."

"I just wish I hadn't wasted all week being so stupid," Todd said humbly. "I still can't believe it was you who wrote me such a great poem. It's like there's a whole other Elizabeth inside that I hadn't seen before."

Elizabeth groaned and covered her face with the wildflowers. "Judging from how you reacted to her, I think I'll just keep her buried from now on."

"No, no," Todd protested. "Just—you know, give me some warning when she's about to come out."

Elizabeth laughed.

"Elizabeth, I just want to say that everything you said in your poem, well, it goes for me, too," Todd said softly. Then he leaned over and kissed her cheek.

Elizabeth smiled and blushed, her heart thumping hard. "Happy Valentine's Day, Todd."

"Happy Valentine's Day, Elizabeth."

"I thought we were finally rid of that boring guy," Jessica said with a sigh as she and Aaron, sitting on the school steps, watched Elizabeth and Todd get into the Wilkinses' station wagon. "But it looks like he sucked her back into his trap again."

"Oh, come on, Todd isn't bad," Aaron said. "Who would you rather have Elizabeth like: Todd, or Bruce Patman?"

"Eww!" Jessica exclaimed, wrinkling her nose. "Remind me to be extra nice to Todd when I see him."

Aaron laughed. "So you liked the cheer today, huh?"

"It was fabulous," Jessica said, beaming. "It was so sweet of you."

"I meant every word," Aaron declared. "In fact, I'm thinking that maybe I should get the name Jessica tattooed on my arm."

Jessica made a ladylike gagging sound. "How

about getting some brains tattooed on your head?"

She tapped his head playfully, and he laughed again.

"But I know what you *can* do," Jessica continued. "You can take me to the new movie at the Valley Mall—the one with the totally romantic Melody Power theme song."

Aaron grinned at her. "It's a date."

"This is a great limo," Justin said, smiling across the leather seat at Lila. "It's nice of your dad to ride in the front so we can be alone."

Lila squeezed Justin's hand. "I wanted to tell you—I had such a good time tonight. That is, after you showed up."

"Me, too," Justin said. "Maybe we can get together again sometime. Like for a movie or something."

"That would be fantastic," Lila agreed, smiling. "Only what are we going to do about you? Do you have to be Gray forever to my friends?"

Justin looked thoughtful. "I know—we'll say Gray went to boarding school, and I'm his identical twin, Justin."

"Your last names are different," Lila pointed out.

"Hmm. You're right," Justin said. Then he shrugged. "Well, I don't see any way around it. I guess I have to be Gray forever. Maybe I should even legally change my name to Gray Williams."

Lila laughed. "I'm sorry. I'm ruining your whole life."

Justin gazed at her seriously. "No, you're not," he said softly. "Not at all."

Lila felt a flutter in her stomach. "Happy Valentine's Day, Justin Gray Williams Pratt."

Gray leaned over and kissed Lila gently on the cheek. "Happy Valentine's Day, Lila Ms. Fowler."

We hope you enjoyed reading this book. If you would like to receive further information about available titles in the Bantam series, just write to the address below, with your name and address:

Kim Prior
Bantam Books
61–63 Uxbridge Road
Ealing
London W5 5SA.

If you live in Australia or New Zealand and would like more information about the series, please write to:

Sally Porter
Transworld Publishers
(Australia) Pty Ltd
15–25 Helles Avenue
Moorebank
NSW 2170
AUSTRALIA

Kiri Martin
Transworld Publishers (NZ) Ltd
3 William Pickering Drive
Albany
Auckland
NEW ZEALAND

Created by FRANCINE PASCAL

Follow the adventures of Jessica, Elizabeth and all their friends
at Sweet Valley as twelve-year-olds. A super series with one
new title every month!

Hang out with the coolest kids around!

THE UNICORN CLUB

Jessica and Elizabeth Wakefield are just two of the terrific members of The Unicorn Club you've met in *Sweet Valley Twins* books. Now get to know some of their friends even better!

A sensational new *Sweet Valley* series.

1. Save the Unicorns!
2. Maria's Movie Comeback
3. The Best Friend Game
4. Lila's Little Sister
5. Unicorns in Love
Super Edition: Unicorns at War